CHILD OF DESTINY

By the same author:
Escape From the Darkness

TALES OF MUNIAMMA: 1

Child of Destiny

CONNIE GRIFFITH

AFRICA EVANGELICAL FELLOWSHIP

KINGSWAY PUBLICATIONS
EASTBOURNE

This book is published in conjunction with the
Africa Evangelical Fellowship,
17 Westcote Road, Reading, Berks RG3 2DL

Front cover design by Vic Mitchell

Illustrations by Juliet Baker

British Cataloguing in Publication Data

Griffith, Connie
Child of destiny.
I. Title
813'.54[J]

ISBN 0-86065-595-4

Production and printing in Great Britain for
KINGSWAY PUBLICATIONS LTD
Lottbridge Drove, Eastbourne, E Sussex BN23 6NT by
Nuprint Ltd, Harpenden, Herts AL5 4SE.

Dedicated with love to Geoff,
my husband, best friend, and God's servant.

And to Ann Marie and Kay Marie,
my lovely daughters, and very special friends.

Author's Note

Did you know there are Asian Indians in South Africa? There are. Today they total nearly one million. About seventy-five per cent of these people are Hindus. Their ancestors brought this religion with them from India when they came to South Africa in the late 1860s to work on the sugar cane farms.

In 1896 the Africa Evangelical Fellowship (AEF) mission began work among this Hindu population. Most of the work has been with the labouring class who worship many gods. Today there are twenty-nine established churches among these people, and they have organised themselves into a denomination called the Evangelical Church in South Africa (ECSA).

My husband, Geoff, and I joined the American Council of the AEF in 1977, and we went to South Africa to work with the Indian people. They became our dearest friends. I believe the struggles and joys of their lives need to be told, and that is why I have written *Child of Destiny* and *Escape From the Darkness*. I hope that children will find here a story that is enjoyable to read and encourages them—like Muniamma—to seek after the 'God who makes the sunrise'.

The incidents in the books, although told with fictitious characters, are based on true situations. As you read, please pray for the Hindus of South Africa, the missionaries working with them, and for the Christian Indian Church as they make a strong stand for Jesus Christ.

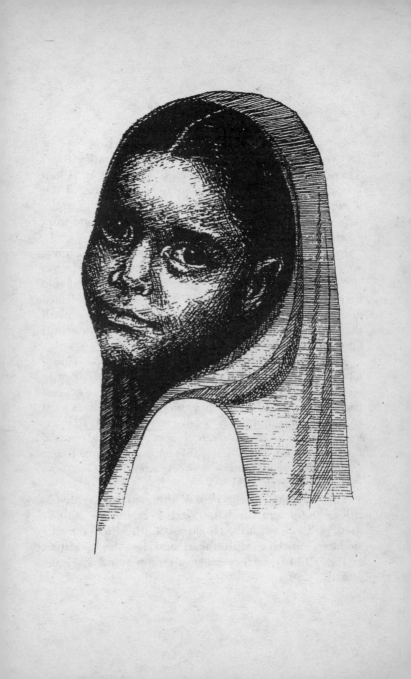

Chapter One

'Where are you, Mummy? Come back to me. Please come back. You can't leave me like this,' Muniamma screamed. Frantically she clawed through layers of gurgling mud. Nothing was left. Nothing. Farmhouse and family had been swept down the valley by the flash flood.

'My brothers,' Muni wailed. 'No! No! Not you too. Why? Why did this happen? Why wasn't I here? It's a curse . . . a curse. There must be a curse on me!'

Muniamma fell face down. Her long black hair fanned around her. Soon it too was covered with mud as she shoved her head deeper and deeper. I want to die, she thought. I want to be buried under here with the ones I love.

Sparky barked. He bit at her blouse. With his sharp teeth he grabbed a huge mouthful of Muni's hair. He pulled. His feet sank but he kept pulling.

Muniamma couldn't hold her breath any longer so she flung her head up out of the filthy grave. Sparky let go and continued barking wildly.

'Over this way,' someone from the rescue team yelled. 'Here's the Indian girl who came with us from town.'

Muniamma screamed and kicked her feet. 'Stay away from me. Go away. I want to stay here.'

'She's hysterical,' Muni could hear someone saying. 'Quickly. Wrap her warmly and get her back to one of the trucks. Make sure that dog stays with her.'

The next Muni knew she was lying on an old cot, and sweet, milky tea was scalding her lips. 'Come on, dear. Wake up. Drink this.'

Muniamma opened her eyes. It felt as if sandpaper was scraping her eyeballs. She stared into Mrs Pillai's brown, frowning face. Mrs Pillai and her husband were owners of a small store in the Indian section of town. 'Come on . . . take a sip.'

Muni gulped as Mrs Pillai tipped the cup. She choked. Her mouth had been coated with mud. The tea and mud mixture sent her stomach reeling. 'I want to go home,' Muni cried as she held her stomach. 'I just want to go home.'

'I know. I know, dear. But you can't. Your home is gone.'

'No! That's not true. It can't be true. I don't believe you.' Muni clutched at her stomach and curled into a ball. She moaned and groaned.

'That sounds like a hurt animal,' Mr Pillai said. He shivered as he walked out of the back room and into the front of the store. 'What in the world are we going to do with her? Where will she live?' he asked the crowd that had gathered.

'She has an aunt and uncle north of here in the

town of Isipingo,' whispered an old town gossip. 'The aunt's name is Sita. She's a Hindu priestess.'

'I'm relieved to hear that,' Mr Pillai said. 'We only knew Muniamma, her mother and the three big sons. It's good to hear she has some living relatives left.'

'Yes,' smiled the old woman. Her toothless grin became hideous. 'In fact, her grandmother lives somewhere in the hills above Isipingo. It's her father's mother. That woman hates everyone. She even hated her own daughter-in-law. I don't think that moaning girl in the back room even knows she has a grandmother.'

'Shush!' Mrs Pillai said, hurrying out of the back room. 'Muniamma can hear you.' Sparky leaped toward the old gossip. He bared his teeth and growled.

'Scram!' the old woman hollered. 'Get that dog away from me or I'll tell everyone about Muniamma's father.'

'Hush!' snapped Mrs Pillai. 'Have some pity.'

'Well . . . the girl lying back there needs to hear about her father and the curse he put on her.'

'Shut up!' someone from the crowd said. 'Muniamma knows nothing about her father. We have enough problems around here without you stirring up old rumours.'

'It's no rumour . . . it's the truth. That girl is cursed. Get her out of here before something else happens.'

Six months later Muniamma was hiding in a banana grove above her grandmother's house. The pain of losing her mother and brothers was still there. It had turned into an aching sadness—a 'lost' feeling. It was a feeling she could not shake off. It seemed as if a dark, thick cloud had settled over her.

'Oh, Sparky . . . Sparky,' she said as she rubbed his straggly fur. He snuggled closer and licked her skinny legs. 'It's too hot, boy. Move over.'

He panted and wagged his tail as he looked up into Muniamma's troubled eyes.

Muni had worked alongside Grandmother all morning. They did the gardening for the Van Niekerks who were white South African farmers. It was lunch time and Muniamma needed to be alone. She wanted to run away but had nowhere to go.

She glanced up at the thick, curved stem of the banana plant which hung almost above her head. It held a bunch of baby bananas. It was already heavy and there were still several weeks to go before the fruit would be ready for Grandmother's green banana curry. So far that was the only good part about living with Grandmother; her cooking.

'She just doesn't talk,' Muni mumbled to herself. 'I can't stand it a minute longer.' She continued rubbing Sparky as tears stung her eyes. 'All she does is yell at me. She doesn't love me . . . she never will.'

Muni slowly turned her head and looked down from the little grove to her grandmother's house. It could hardly be called a real house. It was more like

a cabin—a one-room cabin. The walls were made of dried mud, and years ago someone had painted them white. But now they were a dull grey with dark, reddish-brown stains which came almost halfway up the outside walls. Sparky's muddy paw marks could be seen everywhere, especially under the high, small windows. The sun shining off the rusty tin roof made her squint.

Muniamma closed her eyes for a moment and held her breath. A tear escaped and rolled down her creamy brown cheek and onto her dimpled chin. 'Sparky, I heard what that evil woman said at the Pillais' store. I heard it. I heard my father has cursed me.

'Just look at my skin,' she continued as she shoved her arm in front of Sparky's nose. He began licking. 'I'm dark. I'm darker than most Indians. I hate it!' She jerked her arm away from Sparky's smooth tongue. 'Maybe this is part of the curse.'

Muniamma flopped back against the old banana plant and folded her arms tightly across her bony chest. 'Where is my father? And why would a father curse his own daughter?' she asked herself for the hundredth time. 'I wish Ma would tell me about him. But she won't even mention her son's name.'

Suddenly Muni heard the door slam and looked down towards the house. Grandmother lumbered down the two wooden steps and stood on the dirt path. Muni knew Grandmother was looking for her. She pressed further against the banana plant.

Muni watched as her grandmother thrust her hands on her fat waist. Her swollen, bare feet stuck out from below her loosely wrapped sari. Strands of grey hair had escaped from her thick bun and clung to her flushed face and neck. Grandmother looked around the yard.

'Girl, where are you?' Muni heard her yell. 'Our lunch break is over. We must get back to Madame Van Niekerk's garden. Hurry up, now . . . back to work.'

'Coming Ma,' Muni yelled as she wiped her eyes with the back of her hand. Sparky jumped up and scampered off after a scrawny fowl.

'What's wrong with me today?' she wondered as she followed her grandmother over a small hill into Madame's huge garden. 'Maybe it's because tomorrow is my birthday. Thirteen, and no one even knows. I'm sure Ma won't remember. Oh well, it doesn't matter anyway, does it?' she sighed.

Chapter Two

Later that night the rain started splashing lightly on the tin roof. Muniamma and Sparky snuggled further under the dingy sheet. The kerosene lamp burned low and it cast weird shadows as Grandmother prepared for bed.

'I'm so glad it has cooled off, Ma. Maybe we can sleep better tonight,' Muniamma suggested, hoping Grandmother would want to talk.

'Humph,' Grandmother grunted.

Turning off the lamp, she plopped down beside Muniamma. 'Get that dog out of this bed right now,' Grandmother demanded. 'You know there isn't room for all three of us in here.'

Reluctantly Muniamma shoved Sparky off the side. Whining, he lay down beside the bed. Muni hung her arm over the edge and rubbed his neck. 'Ma, do you know what day it is tomorrow?' Oh, how she hoped Grandmother would remember it was her birthday.

'Of course, it's Friday. You know I always give

offerings to my goddess, Kali, and say prayers on Friday. Go to sleep now. What nonsense you ask!'

The muscles began tightening in Muni's neck. This worship of Kali was the hardest part about living with Grandmother. It was almost unbearable. Muniamma had always called herself a Hindu. She and her mother and brothers were all Hindus. In fact, almost every Indian Muni knew was a Hindu. But Grandmother was different. She was obsessed by one particular goddess named Kali. A chill hit Muniamma. She squeezed Sparky's thick layer of matted fur and held her breath. 'Thirteen-year-olds do not cry,' she reminded herself.

As usual, Grandmother's heavy breathing soon turned to snoring. Even when Muni lived with her mother and three brothers, she never heard such noise. She turned her head to see if the moonlight was bright enough for her to watch Grandmother's lips. It was. She propped herself up on one elbow and leaned closer. First, Grandmother sucked in her pink lips lightly over her darkened gums. Inhaling great gulps of air, her chest rose higher and higher. Then silence. This was the best part because Muni started counting to see how high she could get before Grandmother let out all the air. Once she counted to twenty-three! Then the whole lot came gushing out with lips flapping and sputtering and a gurgling noise deep in Grandmother's throat.

This isn't even fun tonight, Muniamma thought. The smell of garlic was especially strong so Muni

18

leaned back and turned over. 'It's all right, Sparky. I don't even know when your birthday is and you never complain.'

Muniamma sighed as she closed her eyes and hung her arm back over the bed to rest on Sparky's back. Tomorrow Ma is going to make me bow down before the picture of Kali, Muni thought. I . . . I won't look at that picture. I can't. Kali's ten heads are awful. How can Ma worship such a scary goddess? How can anyone pray to a god who looks like that?

'Oh, Mummy,' Muni prayed. 'I can't live without you any longer. Since you died my life is horrible.' Muniamma remembered the slim, tall figure of her quiet mother. Tears dampened her cheeks as she sank into a restless sleep.

Just before sunrise, Muniamma hurried to the out-house. Then, rushing to the backyard tap, she splashed cold water all over her hands and face. Muni didn't want to miss the only moment of the day that brought her peace. It was when the first rays of dawn peaked above the far-off waters of the Indian Ocean, turning them into a crystal blue mirror. It's beautiful, she thought. Just beautiful.

Pulling her eyes away from the distant waves, Muniamma followed the sunbeams as they stretched up across the Van Niekerks' vast cane fields. Finally the first touch of light on the red-tiled roof of the master's home reminded her that she had stood there long enough.

'Get in here, girl, and eat your porridge,' Grandmother grumbled. 'Enough of this lolling around.'

After gobbling the hot cereal, Muniamma ran into the front yard. Grandmother was standing by her Hindu shrine. It looked almost like a miniature house but it was open in the front. It had a shelf in the middle where Grandmother kept the picture of her goddess, Kali.

'Just look at the wood of this shrine,' Grandmother said as Muni approached. 'Some day soon we'll have to repaint it. There is some white paint left in a tin under the bed.'

'Yes, Ma,' Muni said. She stared at the wood, avoiding Kali's picture.

'We have a lot of duties we must do before we can say our prayers.' The worry-lines in Grandmother's brow deepened. 'I've told you before, Kali will not hear us if everything is not done properly.'

Muniamma felt her knees begin to shake. She did not want to bow down before Kali—she did not want anything to do with her. Her own mother had always prayed to handsome gods and beautiful, dancing goddesses. Muni had never felt this fear before.

'You sweep the dirt around the whole shrine area,' Grandmother said. 'Make sure you do a better job than you did last week.'

'Yes, Ma.'

Grandmother reached for the picture of Kali. Her hands trembled as she picked it up. 'I'll take this picture into the house and make sure the frame is shined and the glass clean.'

Muni stared at Grandmother's trembling hands. Then she noticed how Grandmother began sweating. Even the coarse hairs on Grandmother's upper lip glistened. Could Ma be scared of Kali too, she wondered. Muni felt puzzled that Grandmother could worship a goddess she feared so much.

'Oh, no!' Grandmother gasped. 'Look at our milk offering. It's curdled. I must get some fresh milk in this brass bowl right away or Kali may get angry.'

Muniamma watched as Grandmother carried her goddess and the offering into the house. Picking up a small bundle of dried branches she began sweeping. With each stroke Muni got rougher. 'I hate this! I hate this!' she repeated to herself. 'This isn't a birthday at all.'

'Stop that,' Grandmother yelled from the back door. She was drying a vase with a towel. 'You're getting dust everywhere. Now you'll have to clean the shelf of the shrine.'

'Yes, Ma.'

'And take this vase and fill it with marigolds. I want fresh flowers this morning as we say our prayers.'

Muniamma took the vase and headed for the side of Grandmother's house. She loved the bright golden-yellow of the marigolds. This was one duty she did not mind. 'Where is the God who made these?' she wondered. 'I don't believe a goddess as ugly as Kali could make something with such beauty.'

Muni's hands trembled as she neatly arranged the flowers. 'Maybe I shouldn't even think like this.

What will happen to me if Kali gets angry? Ma is going to make me pray to her and I don't want to.'

Muniamma's thoughts were interrupted when Grandmother came out of the house. Grandmother carefully placed the picture of Kali on the shrine and lit incense. The strong, sweet smell filled Muniamma's nostrils.

Then Grandmother picked up a small brass prayer lamp and lit the wick which floated in the hollowed-out base. She lightly put her thumb in a cosmetic jar filled with bright red powder. Smearing this on the top of the lamp, she said, 'That's it, girl, now pray.'

As Grandmother knelt before Kali, she covered her head with the end of her old, cotton sari. Muniamma reached for her shawl and copied her.

Muni kept her head bowed as Grandmother began chanting. Grandmother usually spoke English, but she always said her Hindu prayers in Tamil, her mother tongue.

'I won't look up. I won't look into the horrible face of Kali!' Muniamma determined.

Grandmother continued her whiny chant.

Slowly Muniamma began to feel a force—an awful, cold 'something' pulling her head up to make her look at the goddess. 'No!' she wanted to scream.

Finally Muniamma found herself staring into the face of Grandmother's goddess. Kali was pictured with bluish-black skin and ten heads. Out of each head hung a long, red tongue. Muniamma swallowed hard. A sour taste filled her mouth. Kali had twenty cold eyes. They seemed to burn into Muniamma's soul.

'Help!' Muni wanted to scream. 'Help!' But the words stuck in her dry throat. 'I don't want to keep staring at this picture of Kali,' she thought. 'It looks as if she's trying to grab me. I don't care if Ma worships her, or if her mother did before her. *I don't want to!*

'Can't I ever have any peace, not even on my birthday? Muniamma cried silently. 'There is a curse on me. I know it for sure!'

Chapter Three

Muniamma kept staring at the picture of Kali. Sweat trickled down her back. Grandmother's monotonous chant droned on and on.

Gradually Muni began to feel as though she were floating. She knew she was kneeling on the dirt, yet she had the strange sensation of being above the ground. Her arms and legs no longer felt as if they belonged to her. 'What's going on?' she asked. But she didn't know if she just thought those words or really said them out loud.

Muniamma heard a faint, distant noise. It was the sound of a vehicle coming up the rutted road toward Grandmother's shack. The old truck backfired several times. The interruption seemed to break the spell which held Muni. Her entire body began to quiver as she realised she was once again gaining control of herself. She wanted to turn and see who had come but her muscles would not respond.

Someone coughed.

Muniamma turned her head and looked at Grandmother. Grandmother was still chanting in Tamil and it didn't look as if she had heard anything.

That cough, again!

Muniamma forced herself to turn around and face the intruder. It was Aunt Sita. She was standing by an old, rusty truck, and Uncle was sitting inside. 'Oh, no. Not Aunt Sita,' Muni gasped. 'Why did *she* have to come?' Muni swallowed hard as she continued staring at her aunt.

The last time Muniamma had seen her aunt and uncle was six months before, just after the flash flood. Aunt Sita had wanted to take Muni to live and work in their Hindu temple in the town of Isipingo. There was a huge fight between them and Grandmother. Aunt Sita was a Hindu priestess and Uncle was mainly a lazy drunkard. Sita was a feared woman and was known to possess great powers.

'Ma! Ma! Aunt Sita is here!' Muniamma said with more force than she expected. 'Ma!'

'You know better than to interrupt my prayers, girl. What is it?'

As Muniamma pointed toward her aunt, she noticed Grandmother's back stiffen.

Struggling angrily to her feet, Grandmother yelled, 'Get out of here. Go! You know I told you never to come here!'

Aunt Sita slowly walked toward them. She did not yell back. She just kept walking until she stood directly in front of them.

Muniamma was shocked as she peered into her aunt's face. Her aunt's eyes were gentle, and her expression was kind. She was smiling. Even with rotten front teeth, Aunt Sita's smile was beautiful.

'I have come to apologise, Poonamah'. Poonamah was Grandmother's real name. 'You know, ever since my sister married your son we have been enemies. I am sorry for the way I treated you. Will you forgive me?'

Grandmother looked just as surprised as Muniamma felt.

'What's happened to you, woman? Is this some sort of trick?' Grandmother demanded. 'Why, just six months ago you almost went berserk because I fought to keep Muniamma. You wanted her to work for you in your temple. You probably want her to worship the snake goddess like *you* do. This must be a trick!'

'No, it's not a trick. I have changed. I have become a Christian.'

'What? Are you mad? You have worshipped the snake goddess for years. Besides, only white people are Christians.'

'That's what I always thought, too,' continued Aunt Sita. 'But it isn't true. We can be Christian and Indian at the same time. We can turn to the God of creation and his only Son, Jesus Christ. All I know, Poonamah, is that since I put my life into his hands, I have peace—true peace.'

Muniamma and her grandmother were silent. Their mouths hung open. Finally Grandmother gasped, 'I don't know anything about peace or forgiveness. But I still don't understand you, woman. What is the big fuss? Just add the picture of this Jesus to your shrine next to your snake goddess. You can worship him too.'

'It isn't like that, Poonamah. I have turned my back on all the Hindu gods and goddesses. So has Uncle. We destroyed our family shrine.'

'You did *what*? I won't listen to such foolishness. Not another word!'

Aunt Sita had a tear in her eye as she turned to face Muniamma. Reaching out, she gently rested her thick, worn hand on Muni's bony shoulder. No one had touched her in gentleness since her mother died. The shock made her stomach turn all funny.

'I am sorry, Muniamma, for what your father did,' Aunt Sita said gently. 'It was wrong. But don't worry any more . . . it need not bring bad luck to you.'

'Shut up, woman!' Grandmother demanded. 'She knows nothing of her father. Now get out of here and never come back.'

'All right, I will leave, but I will come back. I'm learning some Christian songs. I want to sing them to you in Tamil.'

'Go on, keep your songs. I don't want to hear any more of this Christian rubbish.' Grandmother turned and marched toward the house. She slammed the door behind her.

Muniamma felt miserable. She didn't know what to do.

'Happy birthday,' Aunt Sita said, interrupting Muni's thoughts. 'I've brought you a small present. It's in the truck with Uncle.'

Muniamma was stunned. She could not say a word as she walked alongside her aunt. Uncle grinned sheepishly from the driver's seat. Somehow he looked different too.

'Here. I hope you enjoy your gift,' Aunt Sita said as she handed Muni a small parcel wrapped in newspaper. 'I can't read but I've heard your brothers sent you to school. This is a little book called the Bible. It is God's message to you.'

Muniamma wanted to thank her but the words stuck tight in her throat. She tried to smile but it felt as if her face was cracking. Oh, how she had missed reading. She had longed to read for the past six months. Grandmother had never learned so there weren't any books in her house.

Muniamma squeezed her only present. It felt so good. It was a book called the Bible—a message from God. Her heart beat faster.

'I wonder if it will tell me about the God who makes the sunrise.'

'Are you still here, Sita?' Grandmother hollered as she came out of the house and slammed the door. 'I told you to leave!

'Come, girl,' Grandmother demanded as she jerked her arm toward Muniamma. 'Let these Christians go home. We have work to do.'

Quickly Muni stuffed her precious gift inside her blouse as she followed her grandmother to Madame's garden. Somehow she knew Ma would hate this new book, the Bible.

Chapter Four

Muniamma hurried to catch up with Grandmother. The little Bible was still inside her blouse and Muni could feel it as she ran. She put her arm down to her side and pressed the small gift close to her waist.

'Ma, what do you think about Aunt Sita?'

'Humph!'

'She smiled at both of us, and so did Uncle.'

'I saw them,' Grandmother said.

'Well . . . what do you think? Could Aunt Sita really be changed?'

'Humph! I didn't believe a word she said. Not one word.' Grandmother stopped at the edge of Madame's garden and turned toward Muniamma. 'Don't forget, Sita is a snake worshipper. She has been for years. You know . . . you've been to the temple with her.'

'Just once, Ma. It was six months ago, after . . . after the flash flood.' Muniamma felt a gnawing pain in her stomach. She couldn't even think about the flood that killed her mother and brothers without those horrible cramps. She clenched at her stomach and the tips of the fingers of her left hand touched the newspaper-wrapped Bible that was hidden under her blouse. She let her fingers rest there for a moment.

'Well . . . didn't you see Sita pray to the snake goddess?' Grandmother asked.

'Yes, Ma,' Muni said slowly. She remembered how she had watched Aunt Sita kneel before her goddess. After a few minutes of Sita's chanting, snakes started to appear. Muni couldn't figure out where they had come from. She just remembered watching those snakes slither up and around and all over Aunt Sita. They wrapped themselves around her waist and finally coiled snugly about her neck.

'Well, girl. Answer your own question,' Grandmother snapped. 'Could Sita change? Could a Hindu snake worshipper become a Christian? No! The answer is obvious. She's a fake. She wants something.'

Muniamma stared at her grandmother.

'But, Ma! Aunt Sita looks different. She seems so much nicer.'

'Humph!'

'I . . . I couldn't believe she asked you to forgive her. Could you?'

'Well . . . that was different. But those were just words. I'm sure your proud Aunt Sita would never stoop so low. She's clever. We must be really careful of her. She probably has some plan to get you away from me.'

This made Muniamma feel a little warm inside. Grandmother wanted her to stay. Maybe Ma liked her—just a little.

'Get to work now. Madame will come out here to the garden to find out why we're just standing around.'

'Okay, Ma. Can I work in the same area as you today?'

'Why?'

'Oh, it's just sort of a special day to me,' Muni mumbled as she hung her head. She kicked a clump of dried mud. When her mother was alive birthdays were always special. Once again she pressed her thin fingers against the little hidden Bible. It was her only gift and she was anxious to look at it.

'Maybe at lunch time I'll be able to sneak away from Ma for a few minutes and read it,' she thought.

Together, Muni and Grandmother walked over to the carrot patch on the far side of Madame's garden. They bent over and began to weed. Muni's thick plait hung almost to her waist. It was shiny from the coconut oil she had rubbed in earlier that morning.

Sparky came bounding toward them with a huge cane rat between his teeth. Its spiny tail twitched wildly into Sparky's face.

'Hey, boy, you found yourself another toy, huh?' Muni teased. 'Madame should pay us extra for keeping down the rat population around here.'

Sparky sprawled out beside her and began to play with his prize. He shook and threw it into the

33

air until the poor rat became senseless. Then, with his paws, he knocked it up and down between the rows of Madame's garden.

Grandmother made a strange noise. It sounded as if she was chuckling and clearing her throat at the same time.

'Your dog has a good idea. What he's doing to that rat is exactly what I want to do to Sita. Why, the very idea of destroying her Hindu shrine and becoming a Christian. . . .'

'But, Ma, I thought Hindus accepted all religions?'

'They do. But if you were born a Hindu you should die a Hindu. This changing of religions is . . . is . . . well, it's just not done,' Grandmother said.

'Do you think Aunt Sita will come back?'

'I don't know. I hope not. But, if she does we'll have to work together. We'll give her trouble — real trouble.'

'Yes, Ma,' Muni said. 'We'll give her trouble.'

Chapter Five

As Muniamma continued weeding she thought over the strange events of that morning. Her only birthday present, hidden inside her blouse, was beginning to feel uncomfortable. She had been sweating, and the newspaper surrounding the Bible was sticking to her skin. In fact, when Muni looked down at her faded blouse she could see newspaper print starting to stain its blue material.

Muni glanced over at Grandmother. Ma hadn't noticed anything. She had finished weeding between the four rows of carrots and had moved over to the cabbage.

Madame Van Niekerk had a huge garden. Most of the food went to feed the dozens of Africans working for Master Van Niekerk in his sugar cane fields. Grandmother was lucky to have this job, and they both knew their boss was kind to allow them to live in the little shack on his property.

Muni stopped working and watched Grandmother for a while. Grandmother always bent over from the waist as she worked, her broad behind sticking right up in the air. She wore an old cotton sari which seldom got dirty in spite of the hard work. Her face was flushed and puffy. Muni had tried to tell her to squat or sit down when she weeded, but Grandmother would only huff at the suggestion.

Sparky came over and stood next to Muni. He had finished playing with the cane rat. His tongue hung almost to his knees as he panted.

'You need a drink, big fellow,' Muni said softly. 'I'm glad someone around here has a good time.' She bent over and ruffled Sparky's fur.

'I wish you could tell me what to do if Aunt Sita returns. Ma wants me to side with her against Sita. Oh, Sparky, I wish my life was as simple as yours. Why can't grown-ups get along?'

The knot in Muni's stomach tightened. She rubbed her tummy.

'Oh, Mummy,' she prayed. 'I miss you so much. Why did you have to die? Why?' Muni sat down in the dirt and hugged her knees.

Once again Muni glanced over at her grandmother. It was almost lunch time.

'If only I can get alone for a few minutes and look at my present,' she thought. Aunt Sita had said it was God's word, God's message to her.

'I'll hide in the banana grove after we eat,' Muni decided. 'I'll read God's message.' She took her arms away from her knees and pressed both hands against the Bible. 'Yes,' she thought. 'Maybe this god will be different from the snake goddess or Kali.

Maybe the god of this book will bring me peace like he's doing for Aunt Sita.'

Muniamma got up and continued weeding until Grandmother called her for lunch.

After the tasty meal of curried cabbage and bread, Muni hurried to the banana grove. Reaching inside her blouse, she took out the small gift. Then for just a brief moment she waited, holding the newspaper-wrapped present tightly.

I want this moment to last, she thought.

Grandmother also hurried to the banana grove and hid. She waited and watched. When Muni was about to open her gift, Grandmother yelled, 'I thought so, you sneaky little girl. Hiding something from me, are you?' She grabbed Muni's present.

Muniamma jumped.

'What are you doing?'

'I'm taking this,' she said as she held up Muni's birthday present. 'I thought Sita gave you something. You've been hiding it under your blouse all day. Did you think I was so stupid I couldn't tell?'

'It's my birthday. Aunt Sita just gave me a present. Please, Ma, give it back.'

'I know it's your birthday. How could I ever forget the day you were born? That's when my son . . . that's when your father. . . .'

'What, Ma? What about my father?'

'Never mind. I'm going to see what you've been hiding from me,' Grandmother said as she tore at the newspaper. Her hands began trembling as she stared at the little Bible. 'What's this? What's this all about?'

'Aunt Sita said it is God's message.'

'Why, the nerve of that woman. This must be the Christians' Holy Book. You listen to me, girl, and listen good. You were born a Hindu and you will die a Hindu. No granddaughter of mine will ever be a Christian.'

Muni had never thought of becoming a Christian. Aunt Sita was the first Indian Christian she had ever met. She didn't even understand what it was all about. All she wanted was to know the God who made the sunrise and to read the book Aunt Sita had given her.

'Please, Ma. Give me back my present.'

'No! Never!' Grandmother's hands began shaking violently. 'I've got to get rid of this book before Kali gets angry. You know she's a goddess of vengeance. But I don't know what to do with it. If it's truly a Holy Book, I have to be careful. If I burn it, something terrible may happen to me. I know, I'll bury it!'

As Grandmother stormed away, Muni wanted to scream after her, 'Give me back my present!'

She slumped down and leaned against the rough stock of the banana plant, her fists clenched in her lap. She hadn't even read one word of God's message to her. In fact, she hadn't even touched the cover.

'Oh, Mummy,' she prayed for the second time that day. 'What's going to happen to me now? How can I keep on living with Ma? Why is she treating me so badly?'

Muni buried her face in her hands and began to cry.

Chapter Six

A week had passed since all the trauma surrounding Muniamma's birthday. Aunt Sita had not returned. Grandmother hadn't mentioned the Bible again, and neither had Muni. They worked silently, side by side, and Muni felt that some of the tension between them was beginning to leave.

It was Friday afternoon, and earlier that morning Muni had helped Grandmother prepare their shrine. She had swept the dirt around the whole area until it was smooth. Grandmother seemed pleased with her work.

Muni had knelt before Kali as Grandmother chanted her Tamil prayers. Muni hated to do this but she didn't want to make Grandmother angry.

Now she and Grandmother were picking lemons and oranges. They were to fill several boxes and deliver them to Madame's back porch. Muni was up in a tree passing the fruit down to Grandmother when Aunt Sita arrived.

'Hello. It looks as if you two have your hands full

today. Here, Poonamah . . . let me help,' Sita said as she came toward them.

'What are you doing here?' Grandmother asked. 'Go on. I told you to stay away from us.'

'I know. But I thought I'd walk up here to help you today.'

'You walked?' Muniamma asked. 'You don't mean you walked all the way up here just to help us? That would take you almost two hours.'

'It did,' Sita smiled. 'Uncle is looking for a job so he couldn't give me a ride today.'

'A job?' Grandmother laughed sarcastically. 'Now that's funny. Your lazy husband hasn't worked in years.'

'I know.'

'He's just been an old drunkard,' Grandmother continued to taunt. 'Looking for a job? That's a joke.'

Muniamma watched Sita. She didn't even look upset at Grandmother's comments.

'It does sound strange, I'll agree,' Aunt Sita said, 'but it's the truth. He hasn't touched a drop of alcohol in months. Now, why don't I start picking fruit from this tree over here?' Sita asked. 'The job would get done a lot quicker.'

'We don't want your help . . . do we, Muniamma?' Grandmother said as she continued glaring at Sita.

Muni was still several branches up in the tree. She answered hesitantly.

'Well . . . no, Aunt Sita. We don't want your help. Ma and I can do our work without you.'

40

'Oh, I'm sure you can. But . . .' That is as far as Aunt Sita got when Grandmother picked up an orange from the box and threw it. The fruit hit Sita in the face.

'Now, get out of here and never come back. And don't you ever bring another one of your Christian Holy Books again.'

'I'm sorry. I didn't think my gift to Muniamma would get you so upset. I guess I wasn't thinking.'

'Yes,' Grandmother snapped. 'You're not thinking straight these days. You're stupid. You've given up so much for this new religion.

'Come on down here, girl,' Grandmother yelled up at Muni. 'Let's chase this mad woman away.'

Muniamma jumped down from the tree. She scraped her wrist on a branch but didn't seem to notice. She felt a giant ball of anger welling up inside her. She grabbed several oranges from the box and started to throw them.

'Get out of here,' Muni screamed. 'I hate you. I hate you. Ma and I are doing fine. Just leave us alone.'

Sita stumbled and fell as she backed away from Muni.

'I'm leaving,' she yelled as she guarded her head from the onslaught of fruit. 'I'm leaving.'

'That's enough,' Grandmother yelled as she grabbed her granddaughter's arm. The blood from the scrape on Muni's wrist was now dripping from her fingers. 'Aunt Sita won't come back any more.'

'Yes . . . yes, I will come back,' Sita said as she painfully pulled herself up. 'I'm going to make you

some home-made bread and bring it the next time I come.'

'You stupid woman. Why don't you just give up. We don't want to have anything to do with you,' Grandmother said.

'I know you don't,' Aunt Sita said as she slowly backed away. 'But I want to have a lot to do with you. I'll come again next week.'

Aunt Sita turned, and as she walked away she began singing. Her shaky voice sounded funny but Muni didn't feel like laughing. The words of the strange song rang out over the top of the sugar cane: 'On a hill far away, stood an old rugged cross.'

Grandmother and Muni stared at the back of Sita until she was out of sight. The ball of anger Muniamma felt as she threw the oranges gradually turned into a feeling of shame. Sparky stopped barking and ran over to Muni. He leaned against her leg. Through misty eyes she looked at her loyal friend. Muni bent over and hugged him tightly.

'Get back up in that tree,' Grandmother demanded. 'Madame will be wondering why we haven't finished picking the oranges. Hurry up.'

'Yes, Ma,' Muni said quietly. She let go of Sparky and climbed into the tree. The scrape on her wrist smarted but had stopped bleeding. Muni stared at the drying blood.

'Come on, pass that fruit down. And stop worrying about Aunt Sita. I don't think she'll come back again. I'd be very surprised if she did.'

43

Grandmother was surprised. Week after week Aunt Sita returned. Often she would bring food and Grandmother made a big show of feeding it to Sparky. Always Sita sang. Muni loved to hear the words of the Christian songs. It appeared as if Grandmother was beginning to listen, especially to the ones in Tamil.

'Oh, Sparky,' Muni said. 'It's been over five months since Aunt Sita told us she was a Christian. I can't believe she keeps coming here to help us work. Can anyone change like that?' Sparky was lying in the shade of the tall mealies, pale yellow corn. His tail flopped up and down as Muni talked.

Muniamma picked up a shovel and started turning over the soil.

'It's awful when someone doesn't fight back. You can't imagine the way it makes you feel.' Muni kicked a clump of mud. 'I don't really think Ma enjoys making fun of Aunt Sita either. At least, I hope she doesn't.'

Sparky looked up at Muni and whined.

'Hush, boy,' Muni said. 'Auntie is helping Ma again today and I want to hear her sing.'

Sparky got up and wiggled over and began licking her toes. The muscles in Muni's neck began to relax. Mopping her forehead, she thought of how sticky she always felt after a heavy rain.

'Stop it,' Muni giggled. 'Shush, I want to hear Auntie's song.' Muni listened as she finished weeding around the tall stalks of the mealies.

Chapter Seven

That night Muniamma felt squashed as Grandmother got into bed and stretched out beside her.

'Either Ma is getting fatter or I am,' she grumbled to herself. Muni turned onto her tummy and flopped her arm over the edge of the bed to rest her hand on Sparky's back. 'I saw Aunt Sita helping you today in the garden. Why do you think she keeps coming?'

'Don't know.'

'It's strange, isn't it, Ma. Did she have to walk?'

'Yes.'

'What did Aunt Sita talk about?'

'Nothing.'

Muni always hoped that on one of Aunt Sita's visits she would bring up the subject of her father again. Often Muni would lie awake at night and think over those few words Aunt Sita had let slip. It had been something about being sorry for what Father had done. Whatever it was, Auntie seemed convinced it did not have to bring bad luck.

Muni turned over onto her back and took a deep breath.

'Ma? Please tell me about my father. Aunt Sita said he did something. I'm thirteen and a half now. I think I'm old enough to know the truth.'

'Not tonight. Go to sleep.'

Muniamma recalled the words of the wicked, old gossip in the Pillais' store. She had said that Muni was cursed—cursed by her own father.

'I think there may be a curse on me, Ma. A real curse. I'm darker than most Indians, and then there's that awful flood. Maybe it was my fault. Maybe I bring bad luck.'

Grandmother was silent for a long time. Muni began to wonder if she had fallen asleep. Finally Grandmother turned over and propped her head up on a pillow.

'Madame Van Niekerk came into the garden and talked with me today.'

'Really?' Muni didn't want to hear about Madame. She only wanted to hear about Father.

'Yes,' Grandmother said. 'Madame told me we can have the next four days off work. She said there is a Christian holiday this weekend. It's called Easter.'

'Did Aunt Sita tell you about this Christian holiday too?'

'No, she didn't say a word about it. She knows better. All Sita does is sing and help me do my work. She's so strange. *Really* strange!'

'I like it, Ma. I really like the song she calls "The Old Rugged Cross".'

They were both silent for about a minute. Then Grandmother said, 'Madame Van Niekerk was trying to explain why Christians celebrate Easter. She said years ago people killed God's Son, Jesus, and put him behind a big stone.'

'No!'

'Yes. She said in three days he came alive again and the big stone was rolled away.'

'Ma, what a story.'

'Then Madame did something real strange. She gave me some chocolate for you.'

'For me? Why would she do that?'

'I don't know. It didn't make any sense. Here it is.' Grandmother reached down under her side of the bed. She held up a small chocolate rabbit wrapped in colourful foil. Muni could see it because of the moonlight coming through the thin curtains.

'What do rabbits have to do with Christians, Ma? Do you think they worship a rabbit god?'

'I don't know. I really don't know. But when she handed me this chocolate she said, "I want to give this to your granddaughter for Easter. I hope you both have a blessed, Holy Season." '

'Why don't we ask Aunt Sita about it? She would know.'

Grandmother laid the foil-wrapped chocolate back onto the floor.

'Go to sleep now. I'm tired. We don't have to work for the next four days and I'm glad.'

'Goodnight, Ma.'

Muniamma felt warm and cosy. Grandmother had talked. It had not been about Father but at least she had talked.

Muni smiled as she turned over and went to sleep.

Chapter Eight

'Wake up, girl. Come on, wake up!' Grandmother grumbled as she shook Muni's shoulder. 'I've already finished saying my prayers and you're still in bed. Just because we don't have to work in Madame's garden today is no excuse for laziness. Up with you and get dressed.'

It was as if Grandmother had thrown a whole bucket of icy water over her. The homey feeling that had wrapped around her like a warm, quilted blanket the previous night was completely gone. In its place was a cold, hollow ache which seemed to lodge around her heart.

'I've decided it's time you heard the truth about your father,' Grandmother stated. 'You've asked often enough. You even asked again last night. Hurry up now, because we have to walk into Isi-pingo.'

Muniamma didn't know why they had to walk all the way into town. What did that have to do with Father? Would they go to Aunt Sita's house? She had so many questions, but she was afraid to ask even one.

Mechanically Muni got up and began brushing out her hair. Her hands seemed to be moving in slow motion as she plaited her long, thick braid. Then she put on her best dress, the last outfit Mother bought. Squeezing the material of the skirt she prayed, 'Oh Mummy, Mummy, where are you? I want you to be here. Do you know what's happening? Ma is going to tell me about Father today. Why didn't you tell me when you were alive? Why? Why did you always keep Ma and Father a secret? Oh, Mummy . . . I'm so scared to hear the truth.'

Muni flopped down on the bed as huge tears started streaming down her cheeks. Sparky came over and leaned against her legs.

'I miss my mother, Sparky. Oh, how I miss her.' Muni's whole body shook with each sob. 'And remember my brothers? I loved the way they always teased me. We had such good times. I just can't keep on living without them.'

Sparky leaned closer and Muni threw her arms around his neck. She buried her face in his fur.

'You stay with me today. Don't leave me . . . please don't leave me. You are the only friend I have in this whole world. Come on now . . . walk by my side.'

As Muni reached the door, Grandmother threw it open.

'Get the rope, girl, it's under the bed. We need to tie this mutt so he won't follow us. Hurry up. Don't just stand there staring at me.'

Muniamma stumbled back. She got down and reached under the bed. She tried to concentrate on breathing slowly because she felt as if she were going to faint.

'What's taking so long? Can't you find it?'

Muniamma just stayed there.

'Hurry up. I'm sure it's under there somewhere.'

Muni grabbed the rope and stood up. 'Ma, please . . . *please* can Sparky come? He won't bother anyone. I'll make sure of it, I promise!'

'No! Town will be really crowded today because of the Hindu fire-walking ceremony.'

Muniamma had heard how devoted Hindus walked on fire without getting burned, but she had never seen it. She had heard how men and women made vows to their gods and then walked on white-hot coals to show how sincere they were. Why would Grandmother want to go there? And what did it have to do with Father?

'But . . . but Ma! *Please* let Sparky come.'

'No! And none of this talking back. Tie that dog up good and tight unless you want to lose him!'

Numbly, Muniamma took Sparky to the back yard tap. After filling his bowl, they walked to the banana grove. The sun was just beginning to peek above the horizon. Muni did not even notice. Making sure the rope was secure, she knelt and squeezed him tightly.

'I'm scared. I've wanted to hear about Father for years, but I don't any more.' Taking his loving face between her hands, she asked, 'If I have a curse on me will you still be my best friend?'

Sparky backed away. Whining, he began yanking at the rope.

'I know, boy. I just wish I was tied up with you today. I have a feeling it would be better than hearing the truth about Father.'

Muniamma's legs felt like rubber as she followed Grandmother through the sugar cane fields. Not one word had been spoken for over an hour. As they neared town, Grandmother halted.

'Okay, girl. Before we go any further, I am going to talk,' she announced between short, raspy breaths.

Muni had been nervously chewing on sugar cane. She wanted to get rid of the mouthful which was threatening to choke her.

'Your father was a terrible man,' Grandmother began. 'It is awful to say that about my own son. But it's the truth.'

Muniamma grabbed the handkerchief she always kept up her sleeve. She held it firmly to her mouth.

'He was our only child,' Grandmother continued. 'I guess your grandfather and I spoiled him. Krish always got into trouble with neighbours, teachers and police. I prayed to Kali every day, and I always made Krish pray too.'

'Krish . . . Krish,' Muni repeated. 'Ma, that's the first time I've ever heard my father's name.'

Grandmother looked sadly at Muni.

'When Krish was twenty-one he came to us and told us he wanted to marry. He had chosen a young girl only fifteen years old.'

'Really? Was she my mother?'

'Yes. She became your mother. But before they got married I talked to her. I told her about Krish's past. I even told her she should wait for her parents to arrange her marriage like Indians have done for centuries. Your mother would not listen.'

'Really?' Muniamma could not imagine her gentle mother being stubborn.

'That's right. She thought the old ways weren't good enough now that she lived in South Africa instead of India. Your mother believed we should copy the ways of the white folk, and marry for love.'

'Really?' Muni repeated again.

'Humph! You listen to me. Don't ever do it. You wait until I choose you a husband, you hear?'

Muniamma gagged.

'Yes, Ma.'

'The first couple of months after Krish and your mother were married, Krish settled down. I thought my prayers were answered and maybe my son would turn out all right. But those hopes only lasted a few short months.'

Grandmother's voice died down until it was little more than a whisper. She stood, staring at the ground.

Muniamma was used to Ma's gruff voice, so this change was scary. A pain started to throb in Muni's temple.

'Then Krish found out your mother was going to have a baby—she had fallen pregnant with your oldest brother. He became angry. No, he was more than angry—he went mad. He slapped your mother around something awful.'

Muniamma felt sick. Her head really hurt. She spotted a few small rocks off to the left of the path and eased herself down. This father of hers, this Krish, used to beat up her kind-hearted mother.

'He's awful . . . he's awful. Why in the world would he be angry about having a baby? I thought all Indian men wanted babies, especially sons.'

'They do. But your father was different. He was a selfish man,' Grandmother continued in her strange, quiet voice. 'He acted worse after the next two boys were born. He drank and ran around doing all sorts of terrible things. Finally the law caught him and put him in jail.'

The pounding in Muniamma's head became stronger. She leaned forward on the small rock and pulled her knees up to her dimpled chin. Hugging her legs tightly, she began swaying back and forth.

'Those eight years Krish was in prison were hard years for your mother.' Grandmother's voice became more forceful. 'But as I told her a hundred times, she was better off without him. I helped her all I could with your three brothers, but my husband got sick and I had to care for him. Finally he died.'

Muniamma looked up at Grandmother. She had never talked about Grandfather before. Muni thought of how alone and totally friendless Grandmother looked as she stood in the middle of the sugar cane. It dawned on her how little they really knew each other. Muni had an impulse to jump up and hug her, but she knew Grandmother hated any display of emotion.

'Are you listening, Granddaughter? You're just sitting there staring at me.'

'I'm listening, Ma.'

'Good, because I don't want to repeat any of this.' Grandmother brought out the handkerchief she always kept down the front of her sari blouse. She mopped her forehead and upper lip.

Muniamma stared at Grandmother's chest. It seemed to be heaving uncontrollably.

'Ma, are you all right?'

'I think I should sit down,' Grandmother mumbled as she lowered herself onto a nearby rock. She looked Muniamma straight in the eye. 'When Krish got out of jail, your mother, being a good Hindu wife, accepted him back. He said he had learned his lesson and was a changed man. He really wanted a daughter to prove how good a father he could be. One day he took a vow. A vow to the goddess Kali.'

The pain in Muniamma's head became so violent it felt as if her skull would crack wide open. Her heart pounded against her ribs. She closed her eyes tightly and pressed her face hard against her knees.

'A vow to Kali? Not Kali. Any other goddess but *her!*' She recalled the picture of this terrible goddess with her ten, bluish-black heads. An acid taste filled Muni's mouth.

'I watched your father.' Grandmother's voice sounded as if it came from a long distance away. 'He went out and bought a goat. He took it to the Hindu temple and with the help of the priest they sacrificed the goat before the image of Kali. Afterwards he made a vow. It went something like this:

"Oh Kali, if you give me a daughter I promise I will change. I promise I will be a good husband and a good father to my three sons and especially to the daughter you give me." '

Muniamma began to take a deep breath. It was not as bad as she had thought. Most Hindus make vows. She looked up feeling a little relief.

Grandmother was still frowning darkly.

'Your father went on to say, "I promise I will walk on hot coals at the next Hindu fire-walking ceremony if you fulfil my wish. If I don't . . . you can curse the very daughter you give me." '

They stared at one another. Muniamma could not breathe. Neither one said a word for a long time. Muni knew the truth without hearing it. Father never walked on fire like he had promised. She was cursed . . . cursed by Kali.

'No, Ma! No! Please tell me it's not true. *Please!*'

Grandmother hung her head, and her shoulders slumped even more than usual. She just shook her head sadly.

'I told him not to do it. I told him not to vow to Kali. What a terrible, terrible curse . . . and on his own daughter.'

'What happened to Father? Why didn't he walk the fire-pit after I was born? Why didn't he keep his promise to Kali?'

'I don't know. The day you were born he left. He ran away. Your mother told me to get out. She never wanted to see me again. She never wanted anything more to do with me or my son, or my goddess, Kali.'

'What's going to happen to me?' Muniamma's voice screeched. 'What's Kali going to do to me?'

'I don't know. But I do know she is the most vengeful of all the gods or goddesses. In fact, thousands and tens of thousands of people in India have died from epidemics of measles and chicken-pox which she has started.'

'Ma, stop! I don't want to hear this. I don't want Kali's curse on me.'

'It's too late. It's been on you for years. Listen to me now. Do nothing to anger Kali. Give her offerings of milk, coconuts, fowls and flowers. And always say your prayers.'

Muni looked down at her nearly-black arms.

'I bet this dark skin is part of the curse,' she thought. She wanted to scream and never stop. Then Muni remembered the flood that took the lives of her mother and brothers.

'Oh, Ma . . . the flood. Do you think the flood was because of me and this curse? Do you think it was my fault?'

Grandmother said nothing.

Aunt Sita's voice echoed faintly from somewhere deep inside. Those few words she had said months earlier seemed to bring with them a little hope.

'Don't worry. What your father did need not bring bad luck to you . . . need not bring bad luck to you.'

'Oh, Aunt Sita, are you right? Can you possibly be right? Can *anyone* break this spell? Is there a god stronger than Kali?' she cried silently. 'I have got to find out. Is there any hope for me at all?'

Chapter Nine

'Come. We cannot sit here in the cane fields all day,' Grandmother said firmly. 'We must get to town. First, I want to buy some offerings for Kali before we go to the temple to pray. Then we'll walk to the fire-pit and watch. We have a big day ahead of us and you have a lot to learn.'

Muniamma didn't want to budge. Thoughts of her father, the flood, Kali and fire-walkers kept flashing through her mind. It was worse than a nightmare. She desperately wanted someone to wake her and say it was just a dream . . . just a terrible dream.

'We must simply take what life gives us,' Grandmother was saying. 'It is all any good Hindu can do. Don't fight against your lot . . . just accept it.'

But Muni did not want to accept it. She wanted to fight. She wanted to hit and scream and stamp her feet. Life wasn't fair. She gritted her teeth and stood up. Her chin jutted out.

'Don't look so angry,' Grandmother said as she

wearily got up and stood beside Muniamma. 'The gods will condemn you to come back in another life and relive all this misery. Just accept it, girl.'

Muni's mind went immediately to Aunt Sita. She had not accepted life as it came. Somehow her life had changed, and so had Uncle's. But Muni knew this was not the time to mention it.

Grandmother turned and headed down the path toward the town.

Muni yelled, 'Ma, do we *have* to go to the fire-walking ceremony? I want to go home.'

'Yes, we must go,' Grandmother said sternly as she turned around. 'I think your mother was always afraid you would hear about the curse your father put on you if you went. By not going she neglected her Hindu duty—and yours. Now you are my responsibility. We will go.'

'But, Ma,' Muni began sobbing. 'I'm feeling sick. I want to go home. My head hurts and besides . . . maybe Sparky needs me.'

'Listen, you stop that right now. You don't realise what can happen to you if Kali becomes angry. Why, I've heard stories about how years ago her followers in India used to sacrifice a young girl to her. They would actually kill a virgin to stop Kali's anger.'

'No!'

'That's right. But today, no one offers her human blood. Many people kill a goat or fowl like your father did. But the killing of virgins was outlawed in India. And, of course, no Hindu here in South Africa would ever try such a thing.'

Muni walked up and stood close to Grandmother. She whispered, 'I'm scared. I'm really scared, Ma. How can I keep living with this curse on me? How can I stand it knowing something awful may happen to me any day?'

'You must. You simply must live the best you can and hope you never anger Kali.'

'Ma, do you love Kali?'

'What? Now that's a silly thought. People do not love her . . . they fear her. Why would you ask such a question?'

'Well, the other day when Aunt Sita came to help us in the garden I heard her sing a song. It went something like this: "Jesus, lover of my soul . . .". She loves her God, Ma. Aunt Sita really loves her God. I can tell by the look in her eyes as she sings about him.'

'I know. I have watched her too. It's strange. I've never seen anyone change as much as Sita.' Grandmother turned and stared out over the top of the sugar cane towards the Indian Ocean. 'I think we need to be careful. This may still be one of her tricks.'

'I wonder,' Muniamma said. 'We've been watching her a long time now and she really is different. Remember when we threw oranges. We even hit her, and yet she never got mad. All these months we've been mocking her, and still Aunt Sita comes back to help us in the garden. She certainly isn't doing it for the money! Becoming a Christian has made her a new person. Remember what she was like when she worshipped the snake goddess?'

'I remember.' Grandmother straightened her sari and pushed a few strands of grey hair back from her face. 'Sita said she now worships the God of Creation and his Son, Jesus. I still say we need to be careful and watch her closely. She may be faking.'

Once again they started walking.

Muniamma asked, 'Could we go to Aunt and Uncle's home after we watch the fire-walkers?'

'We'll see.' Grandmother sounded as if she were deep in thought. 'This ceremony lasts all day so it may be too late to walk home tonight. Besides, the sugar cane fields aren't safe after dark because of all the African workers.'

Muniamma felt a slight ray of hope. Could Aunt Sita's God take this terrible curse away? Her step became a little lighter as she walked into Isipingo beside Grandmother.

They finally neared the temple area where the fire-pit was being prepared. Muni couldn't believe the crowd.

'Ma, where have all these people come from? I haven't seen so many Indians in one place before.'

'They come from all around. Right here in this little town of Isipingo we have the largest fire-walking ceremony in all of South Africa. Stay close by my side. I don't want you to get lost.'

As they walked along the pavement, they passed filthy, makeshift fruit stalls. Men selling bananas, coconuts and grapes called to passers-by.

'Come, buy these beautiful fruits for your offerings.'

'Buy here, lovely fruits for sacrifices.'

Grandmother stopped at one stall. Muni stood behind her listening to the way she bickered over the cost. Grandmother never paid the first price any shopkeeper requested. She loved to argue and always seemed to buy what she needed for less than others.

Grandmother paid for the fruit and the man handed her a large tray which overflowed.

'Let's go and stand in the queue at the temple entrance,' Grandmother said with a satisfied grin. 'We are going to give these to Kali and say our prayers.'

On their way they passed an area where men were selling chickens. Grandmother stopped.

'I would like to offer a fowl today but I don't have enough money. My goodness, look at these scrawny fowls and the terrible prices they're asking.'

'Oh, sick!' Muni complained. 'That lady who just bought a chicken is wringing its neck.'

'I know. I see her. I hate to tell you this, but there are a lot of Indians here who are only interested in making money. Some will go into the temple and steal the offerings. This woman wants to make sure her sacrifice remains before her god. By wringing the fowl's neck she prevents someone from trying to resell it. No one would buy a dead fowl.

'Hurry, now,' Grandmother continued. 'Run ahead and save a place for us in the line at the temple entrance. We must present this fruit to Kali and say our prayers.'

As Muniamma pushed her way through the crowd she detected an awful smell. The closer she got to the temple the stronger it became. It was as if the whole area reeked with the smell of mothballs. Muni noticed that the Hindu worshippers standing in the line at the temple were throwing little crystal rocks onto a fire. The fire was contained in a white marble stand which looked something like a little birdbath. As the rocks hit the flame they would flare up and an awful smell would spew out.

'What are they doing?' Muni asked as Grandmother joined her.

'That's camphor. We always burn camphor at these ceremonies. It's tradition; that's just what we do—grab a few and throw them onto the flame.'

Muniamma reached into the brass bowl by the white marble stand. She took one piece of camphor and threw it onto the fire. The smell made her stomach flip. Grandmother did the same and chanted a prayer in Tamil as the smoke rose up.

'Listen to all this noise,' Muni said as Grandmother finished chanting. Indian music whined from a parked truck. Hindu prayers, chanted poetry and advertisements droned from another.

'Isn't it wonderful?' Grandmother responded with a toothless smile. 'Everyone has so much fun at these fire-walking ceremonies. Do you see what you've missed all these years? After we're finished in the temple I'm taking you to the fire-pit. Then you'll really understand what this is all about.'

It was finally their turn to enter the temple. They reverently removed their sandals. Grandmother walked in first and carried her tray over to the image of Kali. She placed the fruit on the floor at Kali's feet. The smell of incense hung in the air. Prayer lamps were flickering around the crowded room in front of dozens of other idols.

Muniamma's whole body shivered as she watched Grandmother kneel at her goddess's feet. Muni held her breath. Hot tears began stinging around the rim of her eyes. She closed them tightly.

Grandmother tugged at Muni's skirt.

'Get down here, girl. Bow down before Kali. Pray to her. Tell her you'll be good. Ask her not to give you any disease. Come on. Bow down.'

Muniamma knelt. She kept her eyes closed because she did not want to look into Kali's face. Her heart felt as cold as the concrete floor.

'I can't pray. I just can't pray to her,' Muni said to herself. 'Oh, God of Creation. Who are you? Are you the God who has changed Aunt Sita? Are you the God who makes the sunrise? When I think about you as I watch the sun come up, I feel all warm inside. But, in here . . . in front of Kali . . . I'm cold and scared. Please come and find me. Please . . . *please* rescue me from this terrible curse!'

'I'm glad to see you praying,' Grandmother whispered in Muni's ear. 'But we need to go now. Others are waiting. Follow me.'

They left the temple and headed towards the fire-pit. It was fourteen metres long by seven metres wide. A wooden fence separated the pit from the crowd. They pushed their way through until they stood behind the fence watching twelve men prepare the fire. Each man pushed burning logs with a two-metre rake.

'Because this is the first time you have been to the fire-walking, let me explain,' Grandmother said. 'Since today is also the Christians' Good Friday, we want to acknowledge Jesus as another god. The story is told that the people who killed Jesus put a crown of thorns on his head before they hung him on a cross. So earlier this morning someone started this fire with a crown of thorns.'

'Do you mean to say that Jesus, who Aunt Sita sings about, is dead?' A great loneliness filled Muni's heart.

'Well . . . remember what Madame Van Niekerk said yesterday when she gave me that chocolate rabbit? She said something about people killing God's Son, Jesus, and putting him behind a big stone. She went on to say that Jesus came alive after three days. But . . . that's not the point.'

The people standing behind Grandmother and Muni pressed closer. Grandmother turned around and glared.

'Enough. Stop your shoving. The fire-walkers won't be here for at least another hour or two. Humph!'

Grandmother turned toward Muni and continued.

'The point is, some people say that Jesus Christ is the *only* way. Your Aunt Sita would probably agree with that statement now that she's become a Christian. But I believe one must be sincere. It does not matter who you worship or how you worship, just as long as you are sincere. There is an ancient saying: "All rivers lead to the sea." I believe it's the same with religions . . . all eventually lead to God.'

Muniamma thought about this as she watched the men in their sweaty tee-shirts raking the fire. They were trying to make the pit a level pathway of glowing white coals. She looked around the sea of dark, earnest faces. People were crowded onto rooftops, hanging out of apartment windows and perched in trees. Some merely looked curious, but others looked sincere.

Did this mean a Holy God was pleased? Was sincerity enough? she wondered.

'Come,' Grandmother interrupted her thoughts. 'Before this trough of coals is ready, I want to take you to the river. The fire-walkers have been there since early this morning. I want you to see what they do to prepare themselves.'

Together they rushed through the crowd to the river. The devotees were bathing in the dirty water. Each was chanting prayers. Everyone was dancing wildly.

'These people have been fasting for forty days. This helps to prepare them for walking on the hot coals without getting burned,' Grandmother explained.

'How can they do it, Ma? How can they go for such a long time without food?'

'They eat fruit and vegetables at night but nothing during the day. And they are not allowed to eat any meat because, as you know, blood represents sin to most Hindus.

'Watch now,' Grandmother continued. 'It looks as if the worshippers are ready. They're going into a trance. They are being filled with the spirit of their god.'

Muniamma could not believe what she was seeing. Each devotee's body became strangely still and rigid. Hooks were shoved into the flesh of their chests, backs, arms and legs. Then limes, coconuts or brass bowls of milk were hung on the hooks.

Several excited Hindus attached ropes to the hooks. Others placed garlanded images of Hindu gods and goddesses on carts tied to the ropes.

Muniamma stared as each pierced worshipper began to pull his cart with the flesh of his back. They were taking their gods for a walk! Hundreds of people lined the streets to see and touch the burden-bearing devotees.

'Reach out and touch them,' Grandmother yelled. 'Just one touch will mean a blessing!'

As Muni touched the cold, clammy skin of a pierced worshipper, she thought she was going to faint. She was sickened by what she was seeing.

'Is this what Father promised Kali he would do? If she demands this, what in the world will her curse be like?' Muniamma shivered.

'Hurry,' Grandmother said as she pushed Muni. 'The ropes and carts are being removed. Now they walk the white-hot coals. Let's hurry back to the fire-pit and watch.'

Muniamma did not know how much more she wanted to see.

Thousands of Hindus went wild as the pierced worshippers paraded in front of them. Muniamma gripped Grandmother's arm and found she was reaching for hers. The sky slowly turned dark: storm clouds were gathering.

A small trough at the front of the fire-pit contained water. At the other end another trough was full of milk. The first fire-walker stepped to the front of the water trough. A hush fell over the audience. As his bare feet stepped out of the water and onto the hot coals, he screamed and ran the entire fourteen metres to the milk trough.

The crowd pushed, swayed, screamed, and stretched their hands to heaven.

The next man stepped into the water and onto the coals. He danced around twice before racing to the end. His eyes looked vacant yet piercing.

'Oh, God of the sunrise,' Muniamma prayed, 'I saw that look. Is this the kind of worship you want? Does this please you? I wish I knew.'

It began to thunder. Grandmother yelled above the noise, 'If he experiences pain, sheds blood, or gets burned, we will know he wasn't filled with the spirit of his god.'

They stood watching as one after another ran the full length of the fire-pit.

Finally Grandmother tugged on Muni's arm and yelled above the frenzied shouts, 'There's going to be a terrible storm. Let's go.' They pushed their way through the swaying, screaming mob.

Reaching a fruit stall, Grandmother yelled, 'Aunt and Uncle's home is a few blocks this way. We'll have to go there until the storm passes.'

As Muniamma stumbled up Aunt Sita's front steps, she wondered about the storm. It would probably stop before too long. But what about the storm taking place in her heart? Would it ever end?

Chapter Ten

Thunder crashed overhead as Grandmother knocked on Aunt and Uncle's front door. Muniamma remembered her dog, Sparky; he hated thunder.

'What's happening to him?' she nervously asked herself.

Shivering, Muni once again remembered that terrible flash flood. Had it really been a year ago? The memories were still vivid.

'Ma, do you think there's going to be another flood?'

'No, it doesn't look too bad. You shouldn't keep worrying about floods,' Grandmother was saying as the door swung open.

They both stood in the rain and stared. In front of them were two smiling girls who looked exactly alike. They had curly blonde hair which seemed to be attached to springs. It bounced up and down as they giggled.

'Hello. Do come in,' one of the girls said. She had

a very strange accent. Her light-brown eyes looked straight into Muni's dark-brown ones. 'I'm so glad someone our age has come. My name's Sue.'

The other twin said a little more quietly, her voice sounding identical, 'Please, do come in. You're getting absolutely soaked. You're both standing there in the rain!'

'I beg your pardon, Miss,' Grandmother said. 'We were going to our relative's home. Her name is Sita. We must have come to the wrong house.'

'No, this is Sister Sita's home,' Sue said with a huge smile. She stretched out her hand in welcome.

Grandmother frowned as she and her grand-daughter stepped inside. They wiped their feet on the small, hand-woven mat. Grandmother was confused.

'Why did this girl call Sita a sister? What are white foreigners doing here?' Ma asked herself.

'Hurry, Lou. Please go and get Auntie Sita,' Sue said as her twin rushed off. 'You're the first ones to arrive. We wondered if anyone would come because of this awful storm.'

Muniamma looked at Grandmother. They both were puzzled. What in the world was this girl prat-tling about?

Just then, Lou and Aunt Sita came hurrying out of the kitchen. Sita was carrying a dish-cloth and had flour on her chin.

'Oh, what a wonderful surprise!' Aunt Sita exclaimed. 'You must get dry and have a nice, strong cup of tea.'

72

'No, don't bother,' Grandmother stated firmly. 'We can see you're very busy. Besides, we understand you're expecting visitors.'

'Nonsense. You must stay. You can be a big help to me. Uncle has invited our church families for a meal before the Good Friday service. They should be arriving in about an hour.'

Grandmother could never resist helping in the kitchen. She was an excellent cook and was proud of the fact that she still ground her own spices. Grandmother paused for just a moment.

'Well . . . if you really need my help we could stay.'

'Oh, I do!' Sita said. 'But first, some tea. I see you've already met the twins. Sue and Lou, this is Aunt Poonamah and her granddaughter, Muniamma.'

The twins stepped forward and each grabbed one of Muniamma's hands. Their friendliness was a little overpowering, but they seemed genuine. Muni looked down at their fingers intertwined with hers. The white and the brown looked so beautiful together. She had never seen this before. No white person had ever touched her in friendship.

'Oh my,' she thought to herself. 'Should these girls be so friendly?' Muni felt nervous. 'Wouldn't it be wonderful if everyone here in South Africa, the black and the white, would reach out and hold hands like this? Wouldn't it be great?' she pondered dreamily.

'Come with us, Muniamma,' Sue encouraged as she pulled on Muni's hand. 'We'll towel-dry your

73

hair while the aunties fix tea. Oh Lou, doesn't Muniamma have beautiful hair?'

'We've dreamed of having hair like yours,' Lou said admiringly. 'You must be able to sit on it.'

Muniamma felt so strange. She wanted to hide behind Grandmother, and yet she wanted to stay there forever holding hands. She could not remember being treated as special in her whole life.

'Those twins will help Muniamma come out of her shyness,' Aunt Sita laughed. She and Grandmother watched as the girls walked down the narrow hallway and disappeared into one of the bedrooms.

'Sue and Lou and their family are here from England,' Sita explained, noticing Grandmother's curious look. 'They are just two of the children of Pastor and Mrs Morton, our new missionaries.'

Grandmother had noticed how at home the twins seemed.

'Are they living with you?'

'Yes, until the Morton family finds a place of their own. As you know, there's only Uncle and me. We had extra room so we invited them to stay. The Mortons have five children.'

Grandmother was interested. She had known very few white people. But she did know they loved big houses.

Why would this British family come all the way to South Africa and crowd into an Indian's home? Why didn't they stay with whites? Will they eat our curry? Will they think they're better than us? Will they push their religion at us? These questions and more plagued Grandmother as she followed Aunt Sita into the kitchen.

As Muniamma sat cross-legged on the bed, Sue and Lou brushed her hair. She had tried to answer their questions but the words always stuck in her throat. She could see their reflection in the dressing-table mirror.

'It's not fair,' Lou was saying. 'See how pretty Muniamma looks when her hair is wet. Imagine what we'd look like.'

Sue threw back her head and laughed.

'I know what we'd look like: drowned rats!' As they pushed each other playfully, the whole bed bounced.

'They think I'm pretty,' Muniamma thought in amazement. 'How can anyone possibly think I'm pretty? I bet they would run as fast as they could if they knew I was cursed.'

A sharp pain seemed to stab Muni's heart and her thin shoulders slumped. Would she *ever* have peace? Would she *ever* throw back her head and laugh from somewhere deep inside? She let out a long, sad sigh.

'Let's go and have tea,' Lou suggested. 'Sounds good, doesn't it?'

As they walked into the kitchen, Muniamma stopped and leaned against the door frame. She simply could not take in, all at once, the friendly scene which greeted her.

Squatting by the back door were Uncle, a white man and a teenage boy. They were talking as they cleaned fish over a pile of newspapers. The boy yelled over to the twins, 'Hey, you two, look at these beauties. You should have gone fishing with us. Come and clean a few, will you?'

Sue giggled. 'You know the family rule, Kenny: "You have to clean the ones you catch!" Oh, sorry . . . let me introduce our new friend. Muniamma, this is our brother, Ken. Even if he is a year older, don't let him tease you too much. And this is our father, Mr Morton.'

Muniamma lowered her eyes. Feeling completely overcome by embarrassment, she could hardly breathe. They were saying something, but for the life of her she could not pay attention. There was a ringing sound in her ears as she stared at her feet.

Lou handed her a cup of tea. Together they walked over to sit at a small table. It had been pushed right back against the wall. Newspapers were spread out and a pile of fresh vegetables was stacked on top. The twins got busy making salads.

Muniamma glanced towards the new electric stove. Grandmother was standing there frying fish with a white woman who had a young child pulling on her apron. The woman leaned over and started asking Grandmother questions about spices. Muni could hear the sizzle of the hot oil. The fishy aroma made her stomach growl.

'That must be Mrs Morton and the twins' little sister,' Muniamma reasoned.

No one who really looked at Grandmother would say she was smiling. In fact, she looked stern. But

Muniamma noticed that the frown-lines between Grandmother's eyes were not as deep as usual. Muni had a sneaking suspicion that Grandmother was truly enjoying herself.

At the sink stood Aunt Sita with Kathie, the twins' teenage sister. As they washed the dishes, they sang. It sounded as if Kathie was trying to learn Tamil.

Isn't that strange? Muni thought, as she stared at Kathie's long, auburn hair. Now why would any white girl want to learn an Indian language?

Settling back onto the wooden chair, Muniamma touched her cold fingers to her hot face. This scene was so different from what she had watched earlier at the Hindu ceremony. A chill shook her entire body as she recalled touching the deathly-cold skin of a fire-walker.

She remembered Sue said church people were coming to have a meal and a Good Friday service.

Oh, no, she thought. What is it going to be like? Will I have to watch more people stick pins and hooks into their bodies?

It was therefore totally unexpected when a warm, cosy feeling started to envelop her. It began in her face and reached down to her little toe. She felt as if someone had placed loving arms around her. Beginning to relax, Muniamma picked up a peeled beet and began grating it for a salad.

An hour later a group of thirty or more Indians were crowded into Aunt and Uncle's small home.

Everyone seemed happy to see each other, and some of the women even hugged and kissed as they met. This looked funny to Muni as she watched, because each woman was carrying her family's curry meal in a large, covered aluminium pot all wrapped up tightly in newspaper and dish-towels or even sheets. She knew they were just trying to keep their meals warm, but still it looked odd. As the women met they hugged each other regardless of the large loads balanced in one arm.

The twins tried to introduce Muniamma to everyone, but all she wanted to do was stand back against the wall and continue watching. When she glanced into the kitchen she was certain she saw Grandmother smiling as she piled the fried fish on a platter. Muni was shocked as she watched her Grandmother enjoying herself among all these Christians. It was unbelievable.

The women arranged all the different curries on Aunt Sita's kitchen table. Three huge bowls of steaming rice were added, and also the salads that she and the twins had made. Everyone quieted down and Uncle asked another Indian man if he would pray and thank God for the food.

Muni watched as the man came forward and reverently bowed his head. She noticed his expression as he prayed. It looked as if he really knew the God he was praying to and even loved him.

After the short prayer the women started dishing up the food and passing it over to the men. Then the ladies fixed plates for the children and made sure everyone was satisfied. Finally they served themselves.

Sue walked over to Muni.

'Come with us, Muniamma. All of us kids are going down to one of the bedrooms. We'll crowd onto the bed, and some of us will have to sit on the floor to eat.'

As Muni followed Sue down the hallway, she asked, 'Sue? Do you always call young people "kids" in your country?'

'Sometimes,' Sue said. 'Why? Don't you say that here in South Africa?'

'No. I've never heard people called "kids" before . . . only goats.'

'Really? Come on, I'm starved. This curry smells fantastic!' They hurried into the bedroom, and several young people moved over and made room for them on the bed.

'Hey, Kenny,' Sue called across the room to her brother. He was sitting on the floor leaning up against an old wardrobe with four Indian boys. 'You're neater today. It looks as if you're finally learning how to eat.'

Everyone laughed.

Lou leaned over to Muni.

'You see, Muniamma, we've never eaten with our fingers before like you do. Well . . . sometimes we've used our fingers, but mostly we use a knife, fork or spoon. Now we're learning how to eat Indian style.'

'Yes, and Kenny looks more like he's making a mess than anything,' Sue teased.

'I wouldn't talk if I were you,' Ken laughed. 'You don't do so well yourself.'

'Come on,' Kathie interrupted. 'Enough teasing. Isn't this chicken curry good? It's spicy-hot, but I like it this way.'

'Have you tasted Auntie Poonamah's fried fish?' someone on the other side of the bed asked. 'It's great!'

Muniamma felt proud.

Everyone settled down and started eating. Muni couldn't stop staring at the way the Mortons tried to eat with their fingers. They looked so awkward. It really was especially funny when Kenny bit into a green chilli in the grated beetroot salad.

'Help!' he yelled. 'My mouth's burning! That salad's hot.'

'I know,' laughed one of his friends. 'It's good. You've got to have chillis in a beet salad. Who made it?'

Sue looked over at Muni. 'Well . . . Lou and I made the grated carrot and onion salads and Muniamma made that beet one.'

'It's good,' said the boy to Muni. He looked right at her and smiled. He was about fourteen and Muniamma thought he was really handsome. His shiny coal-black hair was combed neatly to the side, and he had light-brown skin.

Muni almost choked on a piece of chicken. She lowered her eyes and stared at her plate.

'Thank you very much,' she whispered.

Everyone finished eating, and the girls collected the plates and carried them into the kitchen. Muniamma smiled to herself as she reached the kitchen door. The women were talking loudly and laughing as they cleared away the food. Even Mrs Morton was busy working as the twins' little sister hung onto her skirt. Muniamma watched as Grandmother bent over and smiled at the little missionary girl.

'What's her name?' Grandmother asked Mrs Morton.

'Oh, this little beauty's name is Shelley.'

'Shelley,' Grandmother repeated slowly. 'She's a good little girl.'

'Thank you very much, Poonamah. What a nice compliment. I've been watching your granddaughter too. She's certainly a shy young lady, and so sweet. I'm glad she's the twins' age. They'll have lots of fun together. My husband and I have been praying for our children's adjustment here in Africa. We've prayed that God would give them some nice friends.'

'Oh,' Grandmother said. She looked stunned. 'You've been praying for something like that?'

'Yes. Of course we have. You know, God really cares about all these things. He's interested in every detail of our lives.'

'Oh,' Grandmother repeated.

Muniamma watched as Grandmother walked back to the stove to wipe off the grease. Muni wondered about this God of the Christians. He seemed so wonderful.

Then Muni backed up against the wall and watched the men as they began moving the furniture. They were shoving it all back against the walls. Some of the younger men were carrying in wooden benches from the storage shed. Muniamma could hear Uncle talking to an Indian man who wore an expensive-looking, pin-striped suit.

'It was no bother at all,' Uncle was saying. 'We needed more benches for our church services. I was happy to make them.'

This neatly dressed man looked odd standing next to Uncle, who wore a pair of old, baggy slacks. The man in the suit said, 'Brother, the next time you make benches, call me. I would enjoy helping.'

Muniamma noticed something. Some of these people were rich—others were poor. Some were Tamil—others were of different Indian groups. They loved one another. Their differences didn't seem to matter.

Everyone started coming into the lounge. The men sat on one side and the women on the other. Sue and Lou hurried over and quietly whispered, 'Come with us, Muniamma. We want to sit on the floor right in front. Daddy's speaking tonight.'

Muniamma did not know if she should go with them. She felt panic starting to rise in her as she looked around for Grandmother.

Grandmother was sitting with Aunt Sita off to the left. Her back was as straight as a ramrod as she sat on the edge of her chair.

'Go ahead, girl,' Grandmother nodded. 'We have to stay anyway. The storm isn't over.'

As the girls settled into their places, a middle-aged good-looking Indian man stood up. He had a full beard and neat moustache.

'Let's begin our Good Friday service with a word of prayer,' he said.

Muniamma peeked around. She watched the ladies place the ends of their saris over their bowed heads.

'Dear loving Father,' he began, 'we humbly come into your presence. Tonight we want to remember how Jesus died on that old rugged cross.'

Muni could not listen to the rest of his prayer. He had called his God a dear loving Father. She had never known a father, much less a loving father. And there it was again. 'The Old Rugged Cross', just like in the song Aunt Sita often sang.

What could it mean, she wondered. Muniamma determined to listen very carefully.

Chapter Eleven

'As I announced,' said the leader when the prayer was finished, 'we will begin our Good Friday service by singing one of my favourite songs: "The Old Rugged Cross" .'

Muniamma settled into her most comfortable position, cross-legged. Leaning forward, she placed her elbows on her knees and her chin on her clasped hands. The twins crowded closer to make room for more young people.

'Let's sing to the Lord,' the leader continued. 'Concentrate on Jesus Christ and the love that sent him to the cross.'

Muniamma peeked sideways at the twins. Their eyes were tightly closed as they sang. Sue had her arms and hands stretched upwards. Lou kept her head bowed and hands folded in her lap.

This was all so new. Muni glanced around for pictures of images of gods and goddesses. There were none.

On the chorus, Aunt Sita's voice quivered off key.

Muni could hear her above everyone as she sang the words, 'So I'll cherish the old rugged cross . . . .'

Muniamma remembered how she and Ma used to mock Aunt Sita. She felt ashamed and bit down hard on her stubby thumbnail.

One song followed another. Some were loud with clapping; others were quiet and solemn. Sue and Lou shared their songsheets, but Muniamma felt too shy even to try to sing along.

When the singing was finished, the leader announced a 'testimony time'. A poor-looking mother stood up with a girl who appeared to be about twelve. Muniamma noticed the girl's radiant smile. Muniamma was anxious to hear what made this girl so happy.

'Thank you, brothers and sisters, for your prayers,' the mother began. 'As you know, my daughter, Vijay, has been suffering for weeks with sores on her legs and back.'

The mother pulled up the girl's skirt above the knee. Muniamma gasped. Lou shuffled uncomfortably. Sue leaned close and squeezed Muni's tightly-clasped hands. They all stared at Vijay's brown legs which were covered with red, scabby sores. Pus oozed from the centre of some of them. The skin on Vijay's legs reminded Muniamma of the wet, scaly body of a reptile.

'About a year ago, Vijay and I became Christians,' the mother continued. She let go of her daughter's skirt and gently put her arm around Vijay's slim shoulders. 'This decision to follow

86

Jesus Christ made our Hindu neighbours angry. They didn't understand. They accused Vijay and me of not being proud of our heritage as Asian Indians. They believed we wanted to turn our backs on our culture and become like the white man. I tried to explain that Jesus Christ is for all people, but they just did not seem to understand.'

The mother stopped and cleared her throat.

'Yesterday, while I was weeding along our fence, a neighbour's boy, who's about seven years old, asked me a very strange question.' The mother paused and cleared her throat again. She looked over at her daughter. She swallowed hard and continued. 'The little boy asked, "Are you looking for it?"

' "For what?" I answered.

' "For the bottle my daddy bought from the witch-doctor," the little boy said.

'I got scared,' the mother admitted to everyone. 'I couldn't believe it. Why did my neighbour buy a bottle from an African witch-doctor and bury it in my garden?

' "No," I told the little boy. "I haven't found the bottle. Where did your daddy bury it?"

' "Oh, right there where you're digging. It must be there. I saw him dig a hole one night and put it in and cover it up."

' "Why would your daddy do that?" I asked the little fellow.

' "It's a spell. A bad spell. He wanted the witch-doctor to put a curse on Vijay because you don't pray to our gods any more. He says you pray to the white man's God." '

Muniamma recalled the many male and female sangomas (witch-doctors) she had seen. The male sangomas usually wore old animal skins around their loins and sometimes a modern sports jacket over the top. The female witch-doctors often wore a long piece of brightly coloured material which they wrapped around themselves. Always they had animal bladders tied to their kinky, matted hair. These bladders, which were usually gall-bladders, were blown up and looked like small, flesh-coloured balloons.

Many times Muni had seen these African witch-doctors walking down the main streets of town carrying a horse-tail switch and a black doctor's bag. She had never seen inside that black bag, but her brothers had told her it was filled with all sorts of evil looking 'muti' (medicine). The black bag contained such things as bones, animal teeth, snake skins and herbs.

Muni's hands dropped limply onto her lap as she stared at Vijay. The mother walked over to where she and her daughter had been sitting, and picked up a brown paper bag. She walked back up to the front and reached inside.

'I continued digging in my garden until I found this.' Vijay's mother held up a small bottle filled with an inky-black liquid. Coiled around the lid of the jar was a small snake skin tied in a neat knot.

'As soon as I saw this bottle, I understood. This whole problem with Vijay's skin became clear to me. These sores'—the mother stopped, leaned over, and pulled up Vijay's skirt—'these sores are caused by the power of the evil one.'

Once again Muniamma stared at those horrible sores. She felt sick to her stomach. She wanted to turn her head away. Yet something inside her made her feel repulsed and fascinated at the same time.

'We don't pretend to understand,' Vijay said. It was the first time the girl had spoken, and Muni liked her gentle voice. Vijay pulled down her skirt to cover her legs, then straightened up. She was tall—almost the height of her mother.

'I'm a Christian girl and I don't understand how the devil can have this power over me,' Vijay admitted. 'My mother and I thought these sores came from something I was eating, or . . . not eating.' Vijay looked at her mother and smiled. 'But now we see that this is a spiritual battle—a battle between God and Satan.'

'Yes,' interrupted the mother. 'We believe God is good, and he is allowing this to happen for some reason.'

Muniamma was confused. She wanted to ask them how they could possibly think their God was good. How could he be good if he allowed such horrid sores? She wanted to turn around and look at Grandmother. But everyone was sitting so quietly she was afraid to move.

'Ever since my husband died,' Vijay's mother continued, 'my neighbours have expected me to turn my back on Jesus Christ. They thought I would go back to my old ways and follow my old gods. But I haven't.'

'That's right,' said Vijay. 'We've both stayed true to Jesus. We know people are watching us and we want them to see the love of Jesus in our lives. If Jesus heals my sores or not, I will love and follow only him.'

'Wow!' Muniamma thought. She had never heard anything like this in her whole life. She could not believe it. This girl had a curse on her just like she did. Yet somehow she trusted her God.

'The reason my daughter and I have been telling you this is that we would like your prayers. We want our new missionary, Pastor Morton, and our church leaders to pray for Vijay.'

'By all means,' Pastor Morton said as he stood up and walked forward. 'By all means. I believe every one of us here tonight has been encouraged by your faith. I know I have. My family and I have come all the way over here from across the ocean to be your missionaries, and *you* have ministered to *us*. This is wonderful!'

Pastor Morton paused and looked around. Muniamma could see tears streaming freely down his cheeks.

'Mother and Vijay, would you please kneel. Church leaders, please come forward and surround these two precious Christians. We are going to lay our hands on them and pray.'

A number of the men walked forward. There wasn't enough room for Muniamma and the rest of the young people so they started scooting back. Some got up and walked over to stand against the walls. Muni quickly glanced back to see Grandmother's expression. Someone was sitting in front of Grandmother so Muni couldn't see her.

'Good,' Pastor Morton said. 'Let's gather around even closer. That's it. Now, let's pray.

'Dear Father,' he began. 'We humbly come into your presence in the name of Jesus Christ. Please forgive us for where we have failed you. Fill us now with thy Holy Spirit.'

Muniamma was, once again, confused. At the fire-pit, the Hindus worked themselves into a frenzy. But these Christians simply and reverently asked to be filled with the Spirit of their God.

'This is so completely different,' she thought.

'We would like to ask,' continued Pastor Morton, 'that you bind the power of the evil one. You are already the victor. The death of your Son, Jesus Christ, on the cross, and his glorious Resurrection from the dead, proves this fact.'

He continued, but Muniamma could not understand it all. The words of Vijay kept echoing in her head: 'If Jesus heals my sores or not, I will love and follow only him.'

Several others prayed, but Muniamma still could not pay attention. She kept thinking about Vijay's words. She couldn't understand how this young girl—someone almost her own age—could trust her God so completely.

Finally Muniamma's uncle began praying. He had always been a quiet man. It seemed strange to hear him pray in front of others.

'Father, we want to remember this family's Hindu neighbours. May they come to know you and receive forgiveness.'

How can Uncle possibly pray for them? They don't deserve forgiveness! Muniamma thought.

Why, they're the ones responsible for Vijay's sores. Why would Uncle want God to forgive them?

'And precious Lord,' Uncle continued, 'may this witch-doctor see that the power of God is greater than the power of the evil one. We ask that he too will come to know you in a personal way.'

Muniamma clenched her fists. Now Uncle was praying for the Africans . . . even a witch-doctor! She could hardly sit there. She wanted to get up and slap Uncle on the face.

After the prayers, the mother and Vijay got up and went back to sit in their places. Everyone moved around to get more comfortable. The twins' father stood up to preach but Muniamma could not listen. Even when Lou read aloud from her Bible the words would not focus in her mind. Muni's heart was pounding so loudly she was certain everyone could hear it.

She kept watching Vijay. She noticed how carefully the girl lifted her long skirt as if its weight was painful. The sores were still there—red and oozing. Muni felt ill. Didn't their God hear them? Wasn't he going to heal those awful sores?

Then it appeared as if Vijay forgot all about herself. Leaning forward, she seemed to hang onto every word of the missionary's message. Her expression changed from pain to peace.

'How can this be?' Muni wanted to scream. 'How can Vijay have peace? How can she trust her God when I'm so scared of mine?'

Muniamma thought of Kali and the curse. Her stomach tightened into a painful knot. Suddenly she felt alone and desperately afraid. She wanted her mother. She wanted to go home. She wanted to hug Sparky. She was filled with questions, questions . . . but no answers.

Yet in her loneliness and fear she could somehow sense someone reaching out to her in love. She remembered experiencing the same feeling earlier in the kitchen when she grated the beets for the salad. She sighed, and her taut muscles began to relax. She could almost hear someone gently whisper, 'Don't be afraid, Muniamma. I love you. I will take care of you.'

Chapter Twelve

'Come on Muniamma, the meeting's over,' Sue said as she gently nudged her.

Muni glanced around. Sue was right. The meeting was over, and everyone was moving about.

'What happened? Did you fall asleep?' Sue asked.

'No. I've been thinking.'

Sue smiled at her. 'Come with us. We want to go and talk to Vijay.'

'Okay,' Muni said as she stood up and followed the twins. They hurried over to where Vijay stood.

Kenny was already there with some of his friends.

'What do you think of all this stuff about witch-doctors?' Ken asked as they approached.

'I don't know,' Sue answered.

'I don't, either,' Ken said. 'I've never seen a witch-doctor before. Have you, Muniamma?'

Muni felt stunned that Ken should ask her a question. She just stood there tongue-tied. Muni was embarrassed because she was certain she appeared really stupid.

'Of course she has,' answered one of Ken's friends. It was the same boy who complimented her earlier on the beet salad. He smiled at her. Once again Muni thought how handsome he looked.

'My name's Raneesh,' he said.

Muniamma lowered her eyes.

'Hello,' she said, timidly.

'I'm sorry. I didn't mean to answer for you, Muniamma. But, Ken?' Raneesh turned his attention back to his friend. 'Everyone has seen a witch-doctor. Where have you been, man?'

Ken laughed. 'In England.'

'Well, just stay around Africa a little longer and you'll see plenty of witch-doctors,' Raneesh responded. Then he turned to the girl with the sores.

'I liked your testimony, Vijay,' Raneesh said.

'Well, thanks, Raneesh.'

'I think it's great the way you are trusting Jesus Christ. You have been a real encouragement to me.'

'To me, too,' Ken said seriously. 'I can't imagine how I would feel if a witch-doctor put a curse on me. I think I'd be scared out of my wits.'

Everyone laughed. Muniamma even relaxed a little. It felt good to know someone else would be scared. She remembered her own curse. It was never far from her mind.

'Well, I've always thought I'd be scared too,' Vijay admitted. 'That's what's so strange. This isn't like me at all. I'm usually a big scaredy cat!'

'Jesus is helping you,' Lou said. 'And I'm sure that he's going to heal you.'

'Thanks, Lou,' Vijay said. She reached out and squeezed Lou's hand. '*I'm* sure he will, too.'

Then Vijay paused and looked around at the crowd of young people surrounding her.

'I was sort of ashamed, though, when Mother pulled my skirt up so all of you could see the sores. They're so ugly.'

Everyone seemed held in an embarrassed silence.

Vijay self-consciously leaned over and rubbed her right leg through the material of her skirt.

'Why, my goodness,' she said. 'That's strange. My leg didn't even hurt when I rubbed it.' Vijay quickly turned around and lifted her skirt. She stared at her legs and gasped.

'What's wrong?' Ken asked. 'What's the matter?'

'Look!' Vijay turned back and held her skirt up to her knees. 'Just look!'

Even the adults heard her excitement.

'Mother!' Vijay yelled. 'Come and see my skin. God's beginning to heal it. The pus is gone and the sores are not as red as they were.'

Muniamma watched as Vijay's mother rushed over, with Grandmother and Aunt Sita following close behind. The adults crowded nearer, and everyone began talking excitedly.

'Touch my skin, Mother,' Vijay cried. 'It doesn't even hurt.'

Everyone became quiet. It seemed as if all the people in the room were holding their breath. They watched as Vijay's mother fell at her daughter's feet. She reached up and clung to Vijay's legs.

97

'It's true, everyone,' the mother said breathlessly as she rubbed her hands up and down Vijay's legs. 'Oh . . . thank you, Jesus. Thank you, Jesus,' the mother prayed out loud as she wept. 'Now I'm certain Vijay's skin will be completely healed.'

'This is indeed a miracle,' Pastor Morton exclaimed. 'Tonight we've seen God at work. Let's hold hands and thank him. Let's be sure to give God our praise. Come on, everyone. Crowd closer and touch each other.'

Sue and Lou reached out to hold Muni's hands. As they squeezed her fingers she realised she was trembling. Muni looked around the room for Grandmother. Grandmother was frowning. Her toothless mouth hung at a strange angle.

'Oh, Ma,' Muni wanted to yell across the room to her grandmother. 'Ma, can you believe the power of this Jesus?'

Grandmother kept staring at Vijay's legs. It was obvious the skin had begun to heal. She shook her head as if to clear her vision. Then she closed her mouth and set her jaw. Turning away, Grandmother marched toward the kitchen.

Muniamma wanted to cry out after Grandmother, 'Don't turn away, Ma. Please, don't turn away. Why don't you want to learn about Jesus? I do. Can't you see he's stronger than Kali?'

After Pastor Morton's prayer, Aunt Sita came over and stood next to Muniamma. With an understanding smile she reached out and put her arm around Muni's shoulder. She drew Muni away from the others.

'Uncle and I have invited you and Grandmother to stay the night. The weather is still awful, and it's too late to walk home anyway.'

'What did Ma say?' Muni asked nervously.

'Oh, she says it's fine. Your grandmother is not too anxious to get out in this rain.'

There was a pause, and then: 'Aunt Sita?'

'Yes, Muniamma.'

'I . . . I learned about Father. Ma told me this morning on our way to the fire-walking ceremony.' Muni stopped talking and hung her head. She waited for her aunt to say something.

Aunt Sita remained silent. Muni looked up and saw a sad expression in her aunt's eyes.

'I'm scared,' Muni whispered. 'I'm scared because of Kali's curse. Can your Jesus take this curse away? Can he? Can he do a miracle for me like he's doing for Vijay?'

'Yes dear, he can. I have so many stories to tell you about what he has done. But . . . I promised your grandmother. I promised her I would not say anything more to you about Jesus. At least, not tonight. She made me promise before she agreed you could stay.'

Muni stared into her aunt's eyes. They were filled with tears. One lone tear slipped out and rolled down Auntie's wrinkled face. Sita did not reach up and wipe it away.

'How can I understand?' Muni asked. 'I'm so mixed up.'

'Don't worry, Muniamma,' Sita said as another tear escaped. 'God will somehow help you to understand.'

'How, Auntie? How?'

'Oh, just by little ways. He could even whisper in your ear if he wanted to.'

'Could he really?' Muni asked.

'Yes, dear,' Aunt Sita said.

Muni smiled as she recalled her earlier experiences of feeling someone's presence. 'Could this God of yours even make me feel like he's hugging me?' Muni asked, shyly.

Aunt Sita bent slightly and stared close into Muniamma's face. She shook her head up and down as she talked.

'Yes, I'm sure he could. God can make you feel his presence in any way he chooses.'

Muni took a deep breath. She closed her eyes for a moment as she thought about Aunt Sita's words.

I wonder, she thought to herself, could this great God really care for me? Could he really come and help me?

'Oh, Aunt Sita,' Muni said as she opened her eyes and once again looked into Sita's understanding face. 'I'm just so scared and mixed up. I have so many questions.'

'I know, dear. But I'm sure some day you will know some of the answers to your questions.'

'Really? Do you really think so?'

'Yes, I believe you will.'

'Even about why my father cursed me?'

'Probably. Even that, Muniamma, will not seem such a mystery.'

'Really?'

'Yes, I believe so. And I also believe,' Aunt Sita said, with real seriousness, 'that your feet will never walk on fire like you saw at the Hindu fire-walking ceremony earlier today. No, never! And I'm equally sure that some day those dainty, little feet of yours will walk on streets of gold.'

Muniamma felt chills run down to her toes as she stared at her aunt.

'I don't understand what you're talking about. I don't understand at all!'

'I know, Muniamma.' Aunt Sita smiled gently. 'But some day I am sure that you *will* understand.'

'I hope so, Auntie,' Muniamma said. 'Oh, I hope so!'

But Muni found this hard to believe.

Chapter Thirteen

The sound of the crashing thunder vibrated throughout Aunt Sita's home. Muniamma buried her head deeper into the pillow and clenched her fists tightly over her ears. The storm brought back such awful memories; memories of a year ago when her mother and brothers drowned in the flash flood.

'I'm so scared,' Muni whimpered to herself. She curled up into a ball until her knees touched her dimpled chin.

'I'm cursed, I'm cursed,' Muniamma cried. 'Oh, God of the Christians, I need you more than ever before. I really need you.'

Muni thought back over the horrible, confusing day that she had just lived through. It was called Good Friday, but from now on she was going to call it Awful Friday.

She clenched the pillow tighter as she thought about how she had to tie up and leave Sparky, her dog and only friend, earlier that morning.

'Oh, Sparky, Sparky,' she cried into her pillow.

'I know you're scared of storms too. I'm sorry I had to leave you. Please keep safe! I'm coming back, Sparky. I'm coming back, boy,' she promised, trying to send him the message over the kilometres of sugar cane which separated them.

Muniamma could hear giggling from Sue and Lou, the missionary twins. They were washing and getting ready for bed in Aunt Sita's small bathroom. They would be finished soon and Muni knew it would be her turn, but she could not seem to move. She had heard too much, she had seen too much—all in one miserable day.

Curling up into a tighter ball, Muni held her breath.

Maybe if I refuse to believe what Grandmother said about Father and the curse, it won't be true, she thought. 'Please don't let it be true,' she cried.

Someone knocked on the bedroom door.

'Muniamma, are you in there?' It was Aunt Sita.

Muni lay still, holding her breath.

'Muniamma, come on. If you're in there, answer me,' Sita said, as she once again tried to open the door. It was locked.

'I'm here. I'm . . . I'm getting ready for bed,' Muni lied.

'It's your turn to bathe. It's late. Hurry. Your grandmother still needs to wash, and so do I.'

Muni swallowed.

'Coming.'

'There's a fresh towel on the back of the toilet for you,' Sita said gently through the locked door. 'You'd better get a move on before your grandmother gets angry.'

Muni slowly got up, and as she tried to stand she saw her reflection in the mirror. She looked awful. Licking her fingers, she smoothed her long, tousled hair away from her face.

'All right,' Muni weakly scolded herself, 'You cannot keep feeling sorry for yourself. It won't do you any good.'

Suddenly she recalled something her mother said years ago when she saw her daughter feeling depressed: 'Pull up your socks.'

'That's it,' Muni said to her own reflection. 'Pull up your socks. So what if your father put a curse on you. So what if the curse is from the most terrible Hindu goddess. So what if . . .' Her dimpled chin began to quiver. 'Come on, pull up your socks!' she said angrily through gritted teeth. Muni's dark brown knuckles turned a sickly grey as she clung to the edge of the dresser.

'All right, now,' she continued, lecturing herself. 'Walk out of this bedroom and don't let anyone know how awful you really feel. Not anyone.' She turned and walked resolutely toward the door.

Just as Muni opened it, Sue and Lou came rushing in.

'I can't get used to bathing in such cold water,' Sue complained, wrapping herself snugly in a warm robe. 'When we were back home in England I never gave hot water a second thought. But now that we're missionaries in Africa I long for a fabulous bubble bath.'

'We really should be thankful Sita has running water,' Lou interrupted. 'I hear there are some

Indian families and a lot of Africans living in the surrounding area, going without. They have to haul every drop.'

Muniamma felt ashamed. She thought of the old shack high in the Isipingo hills where she and her grandmother lived.

'What about you, Muni?' Sue asked, as Muniamma tried to escape down the hallway. 'Do you and your grandmother have running water?'

Muniamma stopped. She did not turn around. Running water was the least of her worries.

'I'm sorry for asking such a silly question,' Sue quickly apologised. 'I can't think properly when I get tired.'

'You're also too nosey,' her twin teased. 'Let Muni get her bath so we have time to talk in bed. Besides, I'm dying to hear what Muniamma thought of tonight's Good Friday church service. And I also want to know what she thinks about witch-doctors and the healing of Vijay's sores.'

'Now who's being nosey?' Sue laughed. 'Hurry and wash, Muni. We'll see you in a few minutes.'

Muniamma continued walking down the hallway. The twins hadn't even noticed she'd been crying. She was going to be able to hide her feelings after all.

While washing, Muni tried to think of a plan. She certainly did not want to talk to the twins about witch-doctors tonight. Nor did she want to talk about what had happened at their church meeting when the Christians prayed for the sores on Vijay's legs.

Grandmother pounded on the aluminium bathroom door. The noise could be heard throughout Aunt and Uncle's home.

'Hurry up in there, girl. Don't take all night. Others are waiting.'

'Yes, Ma,' Muni said, unlocking the door.

'What's taking you so long?'

'I'm finished.' Muni stepped out of the bathroom to make room for Grandmother's large frame. Grandmother had loosened her bun. Years ago her hair had been a handsome black, but now it hung limp and grey.

'It's been a long day, hasn't it, Ma?' Muni said, a little hesitantly. Muniamma, for once, did not feel like talking, but she was so uncomfortable with the strained silence that she blurted out the first thing that came to her mind.

'Yes . . . yes, it has,' Grandmother replied. 'You've seen your first Hindu fire-walking ceremony today. It's too bad the storm started. It cut short our time at the fire-pit. Besides, it also forced us to stay here at Sita's instead of walking home.'

Thunder rumbled in the distance.

Muniamma felt so alone and confused that all she could do was stand and stare stupidly at the worn linoleum floor. She wanted to be alone to have time to think.

'Why are you standing there in a daze? I hope you're not thinking about the Christian meeting tonight. What rubbish! Of all the nerve—Hindus becoming Christians. Why, this is the worst sin. It's just not done.'

Muni kept staring at the worn linoleum. It was strange how she noticed something so insignificant as chipped and uneven floor patterns at a time like this—a time when her whole world was falling apart.

'What in the name of mercy are you staring at?' Grandmother snapped her thick fingers in Muni's face. 'Don't you even think about becoming a Christian. You were born a Hindu and you will die a Hindu.'

Muniamma looked up into Grandmother's dark eyes and scowling face. Ma just didn't understand. No one did.

'Go to bed now. Sita tells me you'll be sleeping with the Morton twins. I don't want any talking. Who knows what foolishness those missionary children will feed into your mind.'

'Goodnight, Ma,' Muni said, determined not to cry.

When she reached the bedroom she discovered to her relief that Sue and Lou were already asleep. She slipped into the double bed and clung to the edge of the mattress. She desperately missed rubbing her hands through her dog's thick fur like she always did at home.

Thunder crashed. She moaned, 'Sparky . . . Sparky, I miss you.'

Sue stirred.

'Huh? Who's there? Did someone say something?'

Muni lay deathly still. She did not want to talk. She couldn't. From deep inside she felt pain. It was almost as if her heart was an open sore; a sore, red and oozing like those she had seen earlier on the legs of the young Christian girl.

What did Vijay say at the church meeting? Muni thought. Oh yes: 'If Jesus heals my sores or not, I will love and follow only him.'

'Oh, Jesus,' Muni prayed silently, 'could you heal the sores I feel in my heart? I ache. I'm lonely and scared, and I always have to cover up how I really feel. Jesus, could you help me too? Could you?'

Soon Muniamma drifted into a restful sleep. She experienced no nightmares of floods, Kali's curse, or even fire-walkers thrusting hooks into their skin. Not tonight. Tonight, for reasons she did not understand, she slept like a babe cradled in loving arms.

Chapter Fourteen

Early the next morning Muniamma woke with a start. She glanced around, expecting Grandmother to be in bed next to her. But instead of Grandmother, two blonde, curly heads rested on the pillows. It was strange how rested she felt, considering the disturbing news and events of the previous day.

Muni leaned up on one elbow and stared at the missionary twins. Their skin looked pale even against the white of Aunt Sita's sheets. Muni thought Lou's temple area and eyelids appeared almost translucent. She could see little blue veins running right below the surface. It was fascinating.

Oh, shame, Muni thought. The sun must never shine in England. These girls definitely need to be out in the African sunshine.

'Good morning,' Sue said from the other side of the bed.

'Oh, good . . . good morning.' Muniamma quickly leaned back and stared unseeing at the ceiling. She felt embarrassed at being caught examining Lou's skin.

'What should we do today?' Sue asked. She didn't seem to notice Muni's embarrassment.

'I . . . I don't know,' Muni said shyly. 'Don't you have work to do?'

'Not today. Do we, Lou?' Sue shook her twin. 'Come on. Wake up, sleepy head. It's still the Easter weekend. Let's do something really fun today.'

'Sounds great,' Lou said while yawning. 'What do you suggest?'

'I don't know yet. But I'll think of something.' Sue jumped up and grabbed her robe.

Lou looked over at Muni and wriggled further under the blanket. 'Can you and your grandmother stay with us? Can you stay for the rest of the weekend? It would really be super.'

Muniamma smiled. It felt so good to have someone her own age really wanting to be with her. She leaned up on one elbow again and said, 'I would like to stay, but . . .'

'Oh, don't worry, Muniamma,' Sue said, flopping down on the edge of the bed next to her. 'Maybe we can help persuade your grandmother.'

Muni almost wanted to laugh at the idea of anyone persuading Grandmother to do anything she did not really want to do.

'It's not that,' Muni said. She wanted to be loyal to Grandmother. 'We might have work to do.'

'I heard you both have the weekend off. I listened when your grandmother told sister Sita.'

'Well . . . yes.' Muni felt stupid being caught lying. 'But I do have a dog. I'm honestly worried about him. He's tied up. We probably have to go home and take care of him.'

Muniamma knew Grandmother didn't care one little bit about Sparky. But *she* did.

'Well, come on, you two,' Sue said, completely ignoring Muni's excuse. She leaped up and clapped her hands. 'Let's go and get something to eat. We can't think on empty stomachs.'

After washing their faces and brushing their hair, the three girls hurried into the kitchen. Aunt Sita and Grandmother were sitting at the table talking with Mrs Morton who was feeding her youngest daughter a banana. The twins' older sister, Kathie, stood at the sink washing dishes.

'Good morning, Mum,' Sue said. She hurried over and kissed her mother on the cheek.

Lou leaned over and gave her mother a squeeze. 'Did you sleep well?'

'Yes, Lou. Thanks. And I'm awfully glad. I felt exhausted last night.'

Sue got down on her knees and began talking baby-talk to her little sister, Shelley.

'And what about you, little sissy? Did you sleep well too?'

Everyone laughed, including little Shelley. Mushy banana fell from her mouth as she giggled.

Muni glanced over at Grandmother and was surprised to see how relaxed she looked. It puzzled her how Grandmother could change so quickly. She remembered their brief talk in the bathroom the night before.

Maybe Grandmother is hiding her true feelings too, she thought.

'There's hot cereal on the stove,' Aunt Sita said. 'Help yourselves, girls. Poonamah made it.'

'And it's the best mealy meal I've ever tasted,' added Mrs Morton.

'I agree,' Kathie said from the sink. She dried her hands and came over to sit at the table. 'You're such a good cook, Auntie Poonamah.'

'Well, gracious, child. Anyone can make mealy meal.'

'Not everyone.' Kathie looked over at her mother. 'Mum and I have tried and it's always lumpy.'

Sue certainly didn't want to stay and listen to a cooking lesson. She jerked her head at Lou and Muni.

'Come on. Let's fill our bowls with this good porridge and go outside and sit on the steps.'

After the girls settled themselves and started eating, Lou asked, 'What's the plan? What do you think we should do?'

'I've been thinking.' Sue lowered her spoon and looked from Lou to Muni and then back to Lou. 'How about going fishing? Doesn't that sound simply fabulous?'

Muniamma was surprised at the daring of her new friends.

Boys and men go fishing, not young ladies, Muni thought. Don't these girls from England know any better? But even with her misgivings, Muni was intrigued.

'That sounds fun,' Lou was saying enthusiastically when Ken, the twins' big fifteen-year-old brother, came toward them. He wore a tee-shirt and shorts, and around his forehead he had a piece of elastic material. Sweat was dripping down the sides of his face, and his arms and legs glistened.

'Hey, we would have loved to have gone jogging with you,' Sue pouted. 'Why didn't you let us know you were going?'

Ken laughed.

Muniamma didn't know what jogging meant, but after listening to Ken's panting she felt certain it was a lot of hard work. Muni couldn't imagine why Sue was so disappointed.

'We thought we'd go fishing, Kenny,' Lou invited. 'Would you like to join us?'

'Yes. That sounds super. Thanks for not being a spoil-sport, Lou.' He looked over and grinned at Sue. 'Besides,' Ken said seriously, 'I want to get to know Raneesh more. I'll invite him to come along.'

Muniamma remembered Raneesh from the Christians' Good Friday dinner and meeting the night before. He was the nice-looking boy who had complimented her on the beet salad. She recalled how he had smiled right into her eyes. Muni stared at her empty bowl. She would like to see him again. She had never thought too much about boys, but suddenly he seemed important.

Then Muni remembered how Raneesh had also complimented the Christian girl who had those awful leg sores. Muni shivered. Her stomach felt a little sick, as if it were doing a juggling act with her porridge.

116

'Hurry up, girls,' Ken said, interrupting Muni's thoughts. 'Get dressed and I'll run over to Raneesh's. I'll meet you out by the shed in ten minutes.'

The twins rushed up the steps and into the kitchen. Muni followed slowly. She couldn't believe how fast these British young people moved. Her life had been so slow for so long and now it seemed as though everything and everyone was in high gear.

Sue was already talking when Muni opened the back door.

'Please, Auntie Poonamah. Will you and Muniamma stay for the rest of the weekend?'

Grandmother smiled. Muni could tell she enjoyed these white girls calling her Auntie. It sounded so respectful.

'Uncle has already invited them,' Aunt Sita interrupted with a smile, 'and Poonamah has agreed to stay.'

'Oh good! I'm glad,' Lou said. She came up close to Grandmother and rested a hand on her thick shoulder. 'Can Muni go fishing with us? It would be such fun.'

'Fishing?' Grandmother was so taken by surprise that she laughed. It was the first time Muniamma had heard it. The sound did not come from deep within. It was just a little surface laugh, but the tone was so enjoyable that Muni looked over at her grandmother with pride.

'My goodness!' Grandmother exclaimed. 'Muniamma doesn't know how to fish.'

'We'll teach her,' Sue encouraged. 'Please, let her come. She can even wear a pair of our jeans.'

'Jeans!' Grandmother's voice had lost its lightness. 'Muniamma will wear a dress. Young Indian ladies do not wear jeans.'

'I have a cotton dress Muniamma can wear,' said Lou, quickly coming to the rescue. 'Then she won't have to wear her good dress, the one she had on last night.'

'I don't know,' Grandmother said, frowning. 'This doesn't seem proper.'

Aunt Sita interrupted.

'Let the girls go. I don't know what harm it could do.'

'Well . . . all right,' Grandmother agreed, hesitantly. 'Go ahead. But I certainly can't understand why you would want to go fishing.'

'Oh . . . thank you, Ma.' Muni was genuinely surprised that Grandmother had agreed. 'I would like to learn to fish, but Ma?'

'What is it, girl?' Grandmother's voice sounded impatient.

'I hate to bring this up, especially now, but Ma, I'm worried about Sparky. Will he be okay? What about his food?'

Grandmother grunted.

'If your dog is all you have to worry about, you don't have any problems.'

Grandmother knew better. Muniamma realised that Grandmother was slyly reminding her she had a lot more to be concerned about than Sparky. She had a curse—the curse of Kali.

Muni hung her head. She desperately wanted Ma to shut up; to hush and not say another word.

'Your dog will be just fine,' Grandmother said, emphasising each word. 'You left him plenty of food and water. Now, don't worry. Go ahead with these twins and try to fish.'

Grandmother laughed for the second time that day. This time Muni did not feel proud, but ashamed. To Muniamma's sensitive ears, Grandmother's laugh had changed to an ugly and wicked laugh.

'Now, girls, don't disappoint us,' Mrs Morton said. 'Bring back some fish for dinner.'

'We'll try,' Sue giggled. She turned to Lou and Muni. 'Let's hurry and get dressed.'

No one else had even seemed to notice Grandmother's sly and horrible laugh.

As the girls rushed from the room, Muni wondered if she should tell Grandmother about the twins' brother and his friend, Raneesh. She was puzzled because Sue and Lou didn't even mention them. It was almost as if it wasn't important.

Muni knew Grandmother would think differently. It *was* important. Young Indian girls were not allowed to be so free around boys. But if she told Grandmother, the fishing trip would probably be cancelled.

Muniamma pulled the borrowed robe tighter around her skinny body and ran down the hallway after the twins.

'I'm not going to say another word to Grandmother right now. Not another word!'

Chapter Fifteen

Sue Morton skipped back to where Muniamma was walking.

'Come on, catch up with the rest of us.'

Muniamma looked up. She could not believe Sue wasn't embarrassed by all the astonished looks they had been receiving. Ever since the little group of teenagers had left the old shack by Aunt Sita's, people had stared.

First of all, it was odd to see whites in an Indian area, to say nothing about two of them being blonde identical twins in rolled-up blue jeans and old flannel shirts. As the little group traipsed down the streets of Isipingo, people stopped. Some pointed; many whispered. Muni could almost hear their curiosity.

They passed a man and his family who were taking down their makeshift fruit stall. Muni remembered walking by it the day before when she and Grandmother attended the Hindu fire-walking ceremony. She recalled how the man yelled,

'Offerings for your gods. Buy here . . . fresh fruits for sacrifices.'

Muniamma looked away from Sue. She did not want to say anything. What *could* she say—'Stay away, Sue, I'm cursed'?

'Come on, Muniamma. What's the matter? I thought you wanted to go fishing with us?' Sue complained.

Muni stared down at her bare, brown feet. Litter lined the streets—leftovers from the crowd of Hindu worshippers. Muni kicked a squashed Coke can into the gutter.

'Nothing's wrong, Sue.'

'Good! Then let's run and catch up with Lou, Kenny and Raneesh.'

That was part of why Muni was feeling so awful; she slowed her step even more. She knew Grandmother would be angry. Didn't Sue realise that boys and girls their age were never to be together without a chaperone?

'I . . . I should probably go back to Aunt Sita's,' Muni said miserably. 'I shouldn't have come.'

'Oh, don't be silly! If you're worried about wearing Lou's dress, don't be. It's an old one. Really, she doesn't mind.'

Muni took a deep breath.

'No, it's not the dress. I like it.' She rubbed the skirt of the green-flowered material. It hung loosely and a little short, but Muni thought the dress was beautiful.

'Come on, Muniamma. You simply look as if you have the worries of the world on your shoulders.

You need to relax more. I hear there is a river right behind the Hindu temple, just up the street. That's where we're going. You'll be able to sit and take it easy once we're there. Maybe Raneesh will help you put the worm on your hook,' Sue teased.

Muni gasped. She hadn't even heard the last part of Sue's comment about Raneesh. Muniamma stopped right in the middle of the street and screamed: 'Not *that* river! I don't want to go *there*!'

'Hey, what's the matter?' Raneesh asked, as he ran back to Muni and Sue. Lou and Ken followed.

'What's wrong, Muniamma?' Lou asked. 'You look as if you've seen a ghost!'

Muni stood still. Her breath came in great gulps.

'I can't explain. I . . . I'm sorry. I just don't want to go to that river.' She covered her face with her hands but her mind could still vividly see the men and women in their Hindu trances standing in the water. She thought of the hooks being pushed and thrust through their skin. It brought back all the smells and sounds of yesterday. Her head began to spin.

Ken frowned.

'This is stupid. What happened, Sue? What did you say to upset her?'

Sue shrugged her shoulders.

Raneesh stepped close. He stood right in front of Muniamma. He did not touch her but when he spoke she felt as if his voice encircled and shielded her. 'I understand. I've been there before. I know your fear of that river.'

Muni's shoulders relaxed a little and her breathing slowed. Just to hear the words 'I understand' meant so much. But *could* he understand, she thought. Could *anyone* really understand what it was like to have a curse put on them by their own father?

'Let's walk over to those trees,' Raneesh suggested. 'The neighbours already have too much to talk about.'

Muni looked up, her eyes clouded with tears. She followed Raneesh, as did the three bewildered Mortons.

'I knew it was dumb to have girls come along,' Ken sighed. He propped the fishing rods up against a tree, then squatted down next to the tackle box.

'Listen, whose idea was this trip in the first place?' Sue snapped.

'Hush, you two,' Lou interjected. 'Can't you see Muniamma is really upset?' Lou put her arm around Muni.

Muni looked around at the small circle. To think that just yesterday she had met them all for the first time. It didn't seem possible. It felt as if they had known each other for ages. Then she remembered her plan to keep her true feelings well hidden.

What a fool I've been, she thought. How stupid to scream like an idiot in the middle of the road.

What was she going to say now? How could she explain her fear of that river? How could she tell these missionaries about Kali; about how petrified she became when Grandmother made her pray to this ten-headed, vengeful goddess? How could she ever tell them about Father and the curse?

She couldn't, of course. She determined not to say another word.

Everyone by that time had followed Ken's example, and they were all sitting in a circle on the slope above the river. Finally, Raneesh stood up and walked slowly down to the bank. He picked up a stone and threw it in. Everyone could hear it plop. No one moved.

Raneesh was standing tall and rigid with his back to them. The muscles in his neck, across his shoulders, and down his arms began twitching. His head jerked slightly to the left.

Ken stood up and took a step toward his friend.

'Hey, are you all right? What's the problem?'

'No problem, Ken.' Raneesh turned around and climbed back up the hill toward them. 'I've just been remembering the last time I was here.' He paused and looked gently at Muni. 'I saw my father go into a trance right down there.'

'A trance!' Sue squealed. 'Really?'

'Tell us.' Ken's voice sounded excited. 'Did he walk on fire? I wanted to come here yesterday and watch the Hindus walk the fire-pit, but Mum and Dad wouldn't let me.'

'Yes,' Sue interrupted. 'We all wanted to come, but we had to stay at Sita's and help fix the dinner for all the church families.'

'Don't get us wrong,' Lou quickly interjected. Her arm was still around Muni. 'We wanted to help, but we were dying of curiosity.'

Sue looked over at Muni.

'By any chance, were you here yesterday?'

Muniamma stared at the ground. She didn't want to answer. To her the fire-walking ceremony had been no matter of curiosity; it was a matter of life and death. She shifted uncomfortably.

Raneesh looked at Muni and then at the Mortons.

'Let's not fish in this river,' he suggested. 'There's a better place, and it's close. We can go right down to the ocean. There's a long pier that stretches quite a long way out, and we can fish from that.'

Muni sighed, relieved that the attention had been drawn away from her.

'Come on,' Raneesh continued. He picked up the two rods that Ken had propped against the tree and headed for the street. 'Ken,' he hollered over his shoulder, 'once we get to the pier, I'll answer your questions.'

'Great!' Ken said, picking up the tackle box. 'Let's hurry.'

As Muniamma and the twins followed, Muni wondered about Raneesh. What was he going to say? Could he really understand how she felt? She was soon to discover.

Chapter Sixteen

Muni swatted the fly which landed on the sleeve of her dress, then leaned forward and grabbed the metal railing that ran the entire length of the concrete pier. The waves were coming in and going out. Sometimes water splashed up over her bare feet. The sea was no place to play the fool. Muniamma had a deep respect for its unpredictability and knew better than to turn her back.

Sue and Lou had their long rods resting on the rail for support. Sue said, her voice sounding muffled against the crash and spray of the sea, 'Why don't you try, Muniamma? It's fun! Just hold on right here with both hands. That's it. Brace yourself. Now you just have to be patient.'

Muniamma held Sue's rod and waited. She had watched Raneesh and Sue bring in fish. Ken was disgruntled because he hadn't caught any, and now his line was tangled in the rocks at the base of the pier.

Lou was looking up at the hills above Isipingo

and not paying attention to what she was doing.

'Look at all those fields of sugar cane, way up there. Isn't it gorgeous!'

No one paid Lou any attention, but Muniamma heard. She too looked up. Lou was right. It was beautiful. Muni scanned the hills to see if she could see the Van Niekerks' home where she and Grandmother worked. Muni counted four houses, spread far apart, with red-tiled roofing. But she could not distinguish which one belonged to her madame.

'Do you live up there?' Lou asked, dreamily.

Muni nodded her head.

'Where? Which place is yours?'

'I can't tell. I've never seen it from this direction before. I've looked down at the sea, but I've never been down here, looking up.'

Ken yelled, 'Hey, watch out, Muniamma. You have something! Look at that rod bend. Reel! For goodness sake, don't let it get away.' Ken threw down his tangled line and hurried over to Muni. 'Here, let me do it.'

'No, you don't,' Sue laughed. 'Clear off, big brother. Let Muniamma bring in her first fish—all by herself.'

'Come on, you can do it,' Raneesh encouraged. 'Just keep it coming. Slow now. That's it. Give it room.'

Muni kept on reeling. Her arms ached, but she was not going to stop for anyone. Her dress clung to her back. Lou stood excitedly by her side.

'I see it!' Sue yelled. 'There it is—there it is! Wow, Muni, do you see it?'

Muniamma didn't answer. She was a picture of total concentration. Her feet slipped slightly and Lou grabbed her firmly around the waist. Muni braced her feet the best she could and continued bringing in her catch.

Finally, Raneesh leaned over the rail with the net in his hand.

'It's a beauty. Bring it up a little more. That's it. We've got it!'

Muniamma stared at the flopping fish in the net. Its head touched one rim, the body bent almost double in the middle, and its tail fin flipped over the opposite edge. Muni smiled broadly at Raneesh, and then around the small admiring circle of friends.

'Congratulations, young lady,' Raneesh teased, and gave an elaborate, fake bow. 'Any time you want to go fishing be sure to tell me so that I can be there with my trusty net.'

The twins started giggling, and even Ken laughed. Muni looked intently at all of them and then down at the fish. She joined in with the laughter and looked up again into Raneesh's kind, smiling face. She quickly lowered her eyes and felt her face begin to flush.

'I think I've had my fill of fishing this morning,' Ken said. 'What about the rest of you?'

Sue giggled.

'Oh, Kenny, you're such a spoil-sport. Just because you didn't catch any. But we have been at it for quite a while and I'm starved.'

'I brought some sandwiches and fruit,' Lou said. 'Sister Sita gave me that bag over there before we left this morning. Why don't we go and sit on the beach and eat?'

'Besides,' Ken added, 'Raneesh has promised to answer our questions about trances and fire-walking and . . .'

'All right,' Raneesh laughed. 'Let's just string all these fish and tie them here so they will stay cool in the water. And then, I'll tell you all about it.'

Muniamma's happiness turned sour. She did not want her special moment ruined by such talk. She sadly watched Ken string her prize fish, and then followed a few steps behind the rest as they rushed to the beach.

'Where was I, class?' Raneesh said, looking around the little circle. Everyone had enjoyed the potato curry sandwiches, and now they were munching on crispy apples.

Ken leaned forward and shoved Raneesh's shoulder.

'You were at the beginning, Raneesh. You really love to tease, don't you?'

'You're just getting back some of your own medicine,' Sue chirped.

Suddenly, Raneesh's voice became serious. He cleared his throat and moved around until he was sitting on his knees.

'Well, to start with, I was born a Hindu. But, about six months ago, my family and I began noticing a big change in our neighbours, sister Sita and

Uncle. As you know, Sita used to be a Hindu priestess. She worshipped the snakes and she never got along with my parents who worship Hanuman, the monkey god.'

'The *what*?' Ken interrupted.

'The monkey god. There are a lot of Hindus who worship Hanuman, whose face resembles a monkey. People believe he is very clever and will help them in their business dealings—and especially during exam time at school.'

'Stop interrupting, Ken,' Sue said. 'Please, Raneesh, go on with your story.'

'Well, one day Sita and Uncle came to our home. Sita apologised to my mum and dad for the way she had treated them. I was there. I couldn't believe my ears. She asked them to forgive her.'

Muniamma dug her toes into the sand. She remembered the time Auntie and Uncle had come to their house to ask forgiveness, the day before her thirteenth birthday. Then she recalled the small present her aunt brought her: the Bible, the gift that had made Grandmother so irate.

Muniamma rubbed her arm where there was still a small scar from the scrape she got from sliding out of the orange tree in a blind rage. That was the time when she and Grandmother had thrown oranges at Aunt Sita, hitting her in the face. Muni stared at her toes as Raneesh continued talking to his enraptured audience.

'We were shocked, I'll tell you,' Raneesh was saying, 'the day Aunt Sita and Uncle destroyed their backyard shrine. I will never forget it.'

He stopped and gazed up into the sky as if even in the remembering he was somehow awed. No one interrupted.

'Sita had a hole by the shrine where she kept snakes. When she prayed, they would come out of their pit and slither toward her. I used to watch. Sita's eyes would roll back and when her body became rigid the snakes would wrap themselves around her legs, arms, and even go round her neck and face.'

'Oh, sick!' Lou shivered. '*Stop!*'

'I hate snakes!' Sue agreed, scooting closer to Raneesh. 'Go on. What happened next?'

'Well, like I said, six months ago Sita changed. One day she prayed out loud so all of the neighbours could hear. Her prayer was no longer to the snakes. There was a complete change. Her prayer went something like this: "Dear God, I now believe in you, the God of all creation, and in your only Son, Jesus Christ. I no longer want to pray to or worship these snakes. I have been afraid for months that if I turn to you my snakes will become angry and bite me. I am no longer afraid. You are stronger than the sting of the serpent. I know I am a sinner. Forgive me in the name of Jesus Christ." '

'Did the snakes bite her?' Ken asked after a long silence.

'No. They started slithering toward Sita and she calmly said, "In the name of Jesus Christ, I command you to go away." One by one the snakes went back to their pit. Uncle poured in poison and covered the hole with a pile of rocks.'

'You're kidding!' Ken gasped. He got up and paced back and forth, kicking sand as he went. 'Are you making this up?'

'It's true, Ken. My parents were shocked beyond belief. They said it was the biggest sin to turn your back on your Hindu gods. They had never heard of a Hindu becoming a Christian. They said this proved that the monkey god was stronger than the snake goddess.'

Ken sat down. His straight, light brown hair which was usually combed to the side, now hung across his forehead and into his eyes. 'It proves no such thing!'

'I know.' This time Raneesh, good-naturedly, shoved Ken. 'I know it doesn't. It shows that God is love and he will forgive sin—even the sin of worshipping his creation instead of himself, the Creator.'

Muniamma stopped wiggling her toes. She stared at her feet which were now completely covered with sand. The God of all creation, she thought. Oh, how I want to know him.

Raneesh moved off his knees and lay down, leaning on one elbow.

'My parents . . . well, all of us, have been watching Sita and Uncle ever since. It's true—you all know it—they really have changed. When they started having church meetings in their house, my parents became even more angry. You see, we can often hear what's going on—the songs, people clapping, and sometimes even the message.'

Lou looked around at everyone.

'Oh, isn't it simply wonderful. What a marvellous testimony Sister Sita and Uncle have. But what about you, Raneesh? How is it that your parents let you come to church when they are so against it?'

Raneesh let the sand run through his fingers. He didn't answer. He cleared his throat and sat up.

'Please tell us,' Ken encouraged.

Muniamma looked over at Raneesh. She noticed the muscles in his face twitching and his head jerking slightly. She remembered seeing that nervous tic earlier, down by the river.

'What is it?' Ken said, impatiently. 'You're keeping us in suspense. Let us in on the secret.'

Sadly, Raneesh looked over at Ken.

'There is no secret. I just don't want to say anything against my parents.'

'Come on,' Sue urged.

'No, I have too much respect for them. But I will say this: they know I am a follower of Jesus Christ and I no longer believe in Hanuman, the monkey god. It has caused some problems.'

The others kept talking. Muniamma wanted to get away. She got up as quietly as she could and wandered off down the beach. Then she walked out onto the long pier and clung to the round, rusty rail. Her hands began quivering and tears started streaming down her soft, earth-brown cheeks.

'Life is hard,' she said to the waves. 'It's hard for me as a Hindu and it's hard for Raneesh as a Christian. There's no difference.'

She stood thinking for a long time.

Finally the sound of yelling and laughing caused Muni to turn and look. She watched the Morton twins throwing sand onto Ken and Raneesh. The boys rolled over a couple of times then got up and ran right out into the water. A splashing fight followed.

Muni took a slow, deep breath.

'Maybe there *is* a difference,' she said hopefully, nodding her head. 'Yes, oh yes, maybe there is.'

Chapter Seventeen

'How about another plate of food, Pastor Morton?'
Aunt Sita said. She scooped rice onto his plate
before he could even answer. 'I'm sure you are not
finished,' Sita continued, as she spooned more fish
curry over the rice.

'Well, I am rather full,' Pastor Morton smiled.

'Nonsense. Come on. There's plenty of food.'

Muniamma felt proud. Her large fish was the
reason for the generous portions.

Aunt Sita continued around the table.

'No more for me, please,' Mrs Morton said, as
Sita came near. The twins' mother pushed her half-
finished plate toward the middle of the table. 'Honestly, I couldn't possibly eat another bite. This is
my third helping already. I've never been so full.
Believe me, the food is simply lovely, but truly I
can't eat any more.'

'Ridiculous!' Grandmother whispered to Muni.

Muni and Grandmother were sitting in the
lounge, away from the others. Grandmother had

never eaten at the same table with men before, and she had said to Sita and Uncle that she was certainly not going to begin at her age.

'Why is it ridiculous that Mrs Morton is full?' Muni whispered back. 'She has eaten a lot. In fact, she's eaten more than me.' Muni picked at the bones on her plate with her fingers.

'Just look at her, girl. She's too skinny. She needs to fatten up.'

Muniamma stared at the trim missionary lady. Then she remembered her tall, slender mother. Muni's head lifted.

'Some women like to stay slim, even after having children.'

'Don't get cheeky with me, young lady. You have one outing with these foreigners and already you're talking back.'

'Sorry, Ma.' Muni pressed a large fish-bone between her fingers until it snapped.

'When you and those young people came back this afternoon, they were wet and sandy and screaming like banshees. At least you still looked decent.'

Muniamma kept staring at the broken fish-bone. Ma hadn't found out about Ken's friend, Raneesh, going with them. I should be thankful for that, she thought. She wiped her fingers on the paper napkin, then leaned back against the soft, sofa cushions.

'Don't just sit there as if you've nothing to do. Get up and clear the table.'

'Yes, Ma.'

138

Muniamma loved the way the detergent in the hot water bubbled. She and Grandmother didn't have hot water in their shack in the Isipingo hills. They always washed their dishes under the cold water of the backyard tap.

Kathie and the twins were drying and stacking. Aunt Sita and Grandmother were putting away the left-overs and Mrs Morton was sitting at the kitchen table with Shelley on her lap.

'Isn't it getting a little late for you and your granddaughter to walk home tonight?' Mrs Morton asked Grandmother.

Muni glanced over at her.

'It is almost dark,' Sita agreed. 'Why don't you and Muniamma spend one more night? You're welcome. Besides, you're still on holiday. You don't have to get back home tonight.'

'Will Sparky be okay?' Muni interrupted. She turned around and let the soapy water drip from her hands onto the floor.

'Yes, yes, your dog is just fine,' Grandmother retorted. 'We've only been away two days.'

'I think we will stay one more night,' Grandmother continued. She turned away from Muni and spoke to Aunt Sita. 'We'll leave some time tomorrow morning.'

Muni had the feeling that if she hadn't mentioned her dog, Grandmother would have decided to walk home that night. She felt certain Grandmother wanted to be away from these Christians, but she did not want to give Muni the satisfaction of caring for her beloved pet.

139

'Oh, good,' Lou whispered to Muni when every-one was busy working again. 'Tomorrow is Easter Sunday. We have an early church service, right here.'

Muni looked over at Lou and whispered, 'Really? Another church service?'

'This is special. It's the day Christians celebrate Jesus' Resurrection.'

'His what?'

'His Resurrection. That's when Jesus rose from the dead.'

'Shush.' Muni nervously glanced over her shoulder at Grandmother.

Lou caught on quickly.

'Sorry, Muni,' she whispered. 'We'll talk later.'

Muniamma smiled shyly and continued washing the dishes.

Early, before sunrise, everyone was up and dressed in Aunt and Uncle's home. Muni put on the dress she had arrived in. She noticed that it had been freshly laundered, and for a brief moment she wondered who had done it.

Uncle, Pastor Morton and Ken moved all the lounge furniture into one of the bedrooms, and carried in the rough narrow wooden benches that Uncle kept stored in the backyard shed. The small house was again quickly transformed into the neighbourhood church.

Christians started coming and Muniamma spotted Raneesh sneaking in the kitchen door. He smiled sheepishly and nodded. Muniamma smiled.

'I'm glad you could stay,' Raneesh said. He came and leaned against the hallway wall where Muni was standing. 'I was afraid you and your grandmother would be gone.'

Muni was genuinely surprised. She looked up at Raneesh.

'You're . . . you're glad I'm here?'

'Yes. I'm really glad.' He smiled kindly.

Sue came up and grabbed Muni's hand.

'Come. The sunrise service is about to begin. Let's sit in front like we did on Friday night.'

Muni passed Grandmother on the way to the front. Grandmother was talking intently with an elderly Indian woman and didn't notice them. Muni settled into her most comfortable position. She glanced around at the other young people. She noticed Vijay, the girl who had the awful sores. She was showing some of the other girls the skin on her legs. It looked completely smooth. The sores were gone.

That isn't possible, Muniamma thought. How can it be? She wished Grandmother would look over and see Vijay's legs.

The service began with singing. Muni remembered how Raneesh had said his parents could often hear the singing and sometimes the message. She felt too shy to turn around and look at him.

When the song finished, Pastor Morton got up and asked, 'Have any of you ever wondered where the Easter egg and Easter bunny come from?'

This time Muniamma did turn around. She looked right at Grandmother. Grandmother was staring at Pastor Morton. It was obvious she was listening. Muni thought of the chocolate Easter bunny Madame Van Niekerk had given them. It was still at home under the bed. Muni wondered if it had melted inside its bright foil. As Muniamma started to listen, she wondered how the missionary knew she and Grandmother were confused about this very subject.

Pastor Morton began, 'I read from a devotional book yesterday morning and for some reason I felt I should share what I learned with you. When the early Christians started to give up certain foods during the season of Lent—a period of forty days before Easter—one food they stopped eating was eggs. When the feast time finally arrived at Easter, eggs were dyed red to remind people of the joy of Christ's Resurrection. Because of the egg's hard shell, it reminded some people of the tomb which "broke open" when Jesus rose from the dead.

'Now, the Easter bunny . . . *his* origin is even harder to trace!' Pastor Morton chuckled. 'Bunnies are known to spend the winter in dark, tomb-like holes and then emerge full of joy and gladness in the spring.

'These are fun traditions, but they have absolutely nothing whatsoever to do with the true meaning of Easter. Easter is the celebration of the Resurrection of Jesus Christ from the dead. It is the victory shout of the Christians! Don't forget the real reason for the season: our resurrected Saviour whose empty tomb shouts to the world, "He is alive!" '

Muni once again glanced back at Grandmother. Grandmother was staring down at the linoleum floor. It was impossible to tell her reaction.

'Good morning, everyone.'

Muniamma looked to the front again to see who had just been introduced. He was a short, very dark Indian man. He wore a three-piece black suit. The bottom two buttons of his vest were undone, and his large belly stuck out over his belt.

'I'm Pastor Moonsami from down the coast. When I was asked to come and baptise the new Christians this morning—well, I was pleased. Yes, very pleased indeed. What a privilege you have bestowed upon me. Praise his Holy Name!'

'What's he going to do?' Muni whispered to Sue.

'Baptise. It's when people go under water to show they are dead to their old ways. They . . . they want everyone to know they are Christians and . . . and . . . shush! Let's listen. Pastor Moonsami will explain.'

Muniamma watched as people walked to the front, indicating that they wanted to be baptised. Aunt Sita and Uncle came forward. Sita was wearing a beautiful white sari and Uncle had on a freshly starched white shirt.

Raneesh stood up and followed. He too wore a white shirt. Muni suspected they knew and had come prepared.

'We will be going down to the sea for the baptismal service,' Pastor Moonsami continued. 'As we walk through town, I am sure we will gather a curious crowd. Do not be ashamed. Jesus Christ will give you courage.'

A man and woman, who Muni had never seen before, stormed into the room.

'Oh no you don't!' they hollered. 'Get over here, Raneesh.' The man lurched at his son and boxed him along the side of the head. 'I swear, no son of mine is going to be baptised—understand!'

'I asked your permission, Father, but you wouldn't give me an answer.'

'This is my answer.' He hit Raneesh again.

Muniamma wanted to grab his hand and make him stop. Tears filled her eyes.

Pastor Moonsami stepped forward.

'I am sorry. We all thought this young man had your permission. Otherwise, we would not have agreed to his going through the waters of baptism.'

'Christians!' Raneesh's father said in disgust. He spat on the floor. 'Go on, get home!' He shoved Raneesh out of the door.

To Muniamma's horror, Grandmother stood up and shouted, 'We're not staying, either. There is no way we are walking through the middle of town with a pack of Christians! Come on, girl. We've heard all we're going to hear. We are going home.'

Muniamma lowered her head and quickly followed Grandmother out of the door.

Chapter Eighteen

Grandmother pushed her way through the curious onlookers who were starting to gather around Aunt and Uncle's home. Muniamma glanced over at Raneesh's home as they passed. His parents were in their backyard with a group of angry neighbours. Muni quickly scanned the crowd to find her new friend. He wasn't there.

Muni silently followed her grandmother all the way out of town, keeping several paces behind. Grandmother was walking faster than usual and her steps sounded heavy.

Soon Grandmother left the road and headed up the fire-breaker line through the sugar cane fields. Muni knew they had at least a two-hour walk to their shack on the Van Niekerks' land. It didn't seem possible that she and Grandmother had left their house on Friday and now it was only Sunday. More had happened in the past weekend than in the previous six months.

Muni felt some relief that Grandmother didn't

want to talk as they trudged along. She could tell by Grandmother's slower and less determined steps that her anger was gradually leaving.

But Muni's wasn't. Her anger and humiliation got stronger and stronger with each step. She was looking forward to seeing and untying Sparky, but after that—what would there be? Nothing! Nothing but hard work in Madame's garden. No friends. No Raneesh. No fishing. Nothing.

Grandmother stopped and sat down on a rock. She leaned forward, resting her elbows on her widely spread lap. Muni hadn't noticed and bumped right into her.

'Sit down,' Grandmother said, wiping the sweat off her face with the end of her sari.

Muniamma did not want to sit. Earlier, she had broken off a stock of sugar cane which she still held in her hands. She hit the ground, rocks, and other stocks of cane as she paced back and forth.

Grandmother looked up.

'Stop!'

Muni knew better than to defy Grandmother's demand. She lowered her arms and started twisting the cane with all her strength.

'Instead of being so angry, you ought to be afraid. Throw that away and sit down.'

Leaning back, Muni threw as hard as she could. The sugar cane went flying and landed about four rows away. Muni plopped down with her back toward Grandmother.

'Now, you listen, girl. Being mad is not going to help; it's going to make matters worse.'

Muni wanted to scream, but didn't. She kept her back turned.

'Just look. This is the spot where I told you about your father. This is where I explained about Kali's curse.'

Muniamma shivered. It was as if cold, clammy fingers suddenly reached down inside and wrenched out her hot, angry heart. Muni looked around. Grandmother was right. This was the exact spot.

'So don't you go marching around being mad,' Grandmother continued. 'Instead, we both need to be careful. We have to show Kali she is still the one we fear. We must prove to her we did not listen to or believe anything those Christians said. Kali may get angry and give you some terrible disease.'

Muni pulled her bony knees up to her chin and wrapped her arms around her legs. She began swaying. Her head flopped forward.

'That's better.' Grandmother reached over and laid her hand on Muni's shoulder. 'Now you look like the girl who came with me to town. You look humble—not haughty or proud.'

But it was not humility she was seeing in her granddaughter; it was the fact that the fight had been knocked out of Muni and replaced by absolute and total fear.

'We must go. We've rested long enough.' Grandmother patted Muni's shoulder and stood up.

As Muniamma slowly followed, she knew that with each step she walked further and further away from a life of laughing and singing and closer and closer to a life of fear and dread.

Long before she and Grandmother reached home, Muni could hear Sparky barking. She wanted to run ahead but did not have the strength.

'He sounds the same,' Grandmother said.

That's stupid, Muni thought. He's not the same, and neither am I. None of us are. We'll never be the same again.

When Muni reached the yard, Sparky howled. He jumped about and wagged his tail. Dried mud hung from his matted fur.

Grandmother went into the house as Muni hurried up to the banana grove to untie her dog.

Sparky leaped up onto Muni and started madly licking her face. She stumbled backwards and kept herself from falling by clinging to his neck. She untied the knotted rope and Sparky began racing in circles around her. Then he made bigger circles all around the banana bushes and back.

'Oh, you silly dog!' Muni said, as Sparky wiggled up against her legs. His hind end was moving so fast she was surprised he could even stay upright.

'Let me get you some water.' She picked up his overturned bowl and headed for the tap. Sparky darted and jumped at the bowl and knocked it right out of Muni's hands.

'Oh, Sparky.' She fell to her knees and hugged her dog. 'You haven't changed, have you? But I have. If you only knew.'

He wriggled out of her arms and ran to the tap. He looked up expectantly.

Muniamma grabbed his bowl and went over and filled it. Sparky lapped up the water so fast she filled it a second time. Then she splashed cold water all over her face and took a long drink.

She stood and looked down toward the sea.

'Sparky,' she repeated, 'if you only knew.'

Later that night when, as usual, Sparky's thick fur was under her hand, and Grandmother's snores rumbled around the narrow bed, Muni lay awake. Faint moonlight filtered through the banana leaves outside and moved across the bed. Even without the kerosene lamp, there were shadows.

The arms of Kali are reaching out to clutch me, she thought, and she froze, shutting her eyes tight.

But then she willed herself to open them. The moonlight was soft, and everything around her was familiar and safe.

'Do not be afraid,' Raneesh and the twins seemed to say to her.

'Do not be afraid,' Aunt Sita had told her.

Gaining courage, she looked squarely at the shadows. Only banana leaves.

She thought of the sweet fruit that would ripen in a few weeks.

'And who made that fruit?' she wondered.

Yes, it was the Creator God she had heard of from Aunt Sita—the loving God who would hold her in his arms as she slept. He was no father who would run away and desert her as her own had done. He was a different kind of Father. And she must find him.

This story will be continued in
Escape From the Darkness,
the second book in the
Tales of Muniamma series.

THE AFRICA EVANGELICAL
FELLOWSHIP

The AEF is an international evangelical mission. For more information about their work please contact them at their International Office, 17 Westcote Road, Reading, Berks RG3 2DL.

The AEF has hundreds of opportunities for both long and short term service in evangelism, church planting, education, administration, medical work, youth work and other practical fields.

Other AEF offices are:

Australia:
PO Box 292
Castle Hill
New South Wales 2154

Canada:
470 McNicoll Avenue
Willowdale
Ontario M2H 2E1

USA:
PO Box 2896
Boone
North Carolina 28607

United Kingdom:
30 Lingfield Road
Wimbledon
London SW19 4PU

Zimbabwe:
99 Gaydon Road
Graystone Park
Borrowdale
Harare

South Africa:
Rowland House
6 Montrose Avenue
Claremont 7700

New Zealand:
PO Box 1390
Invercargill

Europe:
5 Rue de Meautry
94500 Campigny-sur-Marne
France